Praise for MAX AND THE CATS and

"...marvelously entertaining fiction... a colorful, striking sketch... Anyone as yet unfamiliar with [Scliar's] talent should find *Max and the Cats* a delightful place to start."

—*Saturday Magazine*

"[Moacyr Scliar] grafts absurd fantasy onto sharp reality to highlight verities of the human condition. Here his zany, canny dreamscapes assert that Germans cannot hide from the atrocities of WWII and will be compelled by their consciences to confront the Nazis in their midst. This message is seamlessly delivered without hint of polemic through the bizarre, hilarious and poignant antics of one Max Schmidt... Terse and whimsical, this engaging subterraneous fantasy strengthens the writer's already intrepid voice in Latin fiction."

—*Publisher's Weekly*

"...an intriguing blend of magic, politics and personal anxieties."

—*New York Newsday*

"Like Maupassant or Chekhov, Mr. Scliar writes about unwanted anxieties and meaningful experiences with a delicious, distinctive style."

—*New York Times Book Review*

"Scliar may be the best writer to introduce us to the wonderful world of Latin American fiction."

—*San Francisco Chronicle*

LESTER
&ORPEN
DENNYS
PUBLISHERS

Isabel Allende *The Stories of Eva Luna*
Joan Barfoot *Abra*
Joan Barfoot *Duet for Three*
Sandra Birdsell *The Missing Child*
Italo Calvino *Difficult Loves*
Italo Calvino *If on a winter's night a traveler*
Italo Calvino *Marcovaldo*
Italo Calvino *Mr. Palomar*
Matt Cohen *Emotional Arithmetic*
Matt Cohen *The Spanish Doctor*
Don DeLillo *Libra*
Graham Greene *Monsignor Quixote*
Graham Greene *Ways of Escape*
Graham Greene *The Tenth Man*
Kazuo Ishiguro *The Remains of the Day*
George Jonas *Final Decree*
Thomas Keneally *A Family Madness*
Norman Levine *The Ability to Forget*
Norman Levine *By a Frozen River*
Ian McEwan *The Child in Time*
Ian McEwan *The Innocent*
Brian Moore *Lies of Silence*
P.K. Page *Brazilian Journal*
Jane Rule *A Hot-Eyed Moderate*
Moacyr Scliar, *Max and the Cats*
Josef Skvorecky *The Bass Saxophone*
Josef Skvorecky *The Boruvka Mysteries*
Josef Skvorecky *The Engineer of Human Souls*
Josef Skvorecky *The Miracle Game*
Josef Skvorecky *The Swell Season*
Linda Spalding *Daughters of Captain Cook*
Susan Swan *The Biggest Modern Woman of the World*
Susan Swan *The Last of the Golden Girls*
William Trevor *Family Sins*

Max and the Cats

About the Author

Moacyr Scliar is the author of sixty-two works of fiction and non-fiction. He has received numerous international prizes for his works, which have been published in over a dozen languages. Several of his fictional works have been adapted in Brazil or abroad for film, theater, television and radio. He has been a visiting professor and a guest lecturer at various universities in Europe and North America. He lives with his wife and family in Puerto Alegre, where he worked for many years as a doctor, specializing in public health.

Books by Moacyr Scliar

The Ballad of the False Messiah
The Carnival of the Animals
The Centaur in the Garden
The Enigmatic Eye
The Gods of Raquel
The One-Man Army
The Strange Nation of Rafael Mendes
The Volunteers

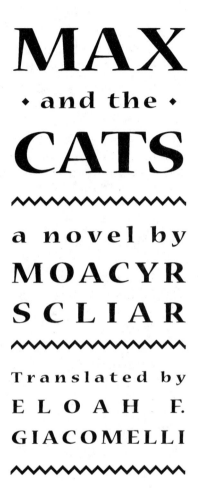

MAX

◆ and the ◆

CATS

〰〰〰〰〰〰〰〰

a novel by
MOACYR
SCLIAR

〰〰〰〰〰〰〰〰

Translated by
ELOAH F.
GIACOMELLI

〰〰〰〰〰〰〰〰

LESTER
&ORPEN
DENNYS
PUBLISHERS

Originally published in Portuguese in 1981 by L&PM Editores Ltda., Brazil, as
Max e Os Felinos.

National Library of Canada Cataloguing in Publication

Scliar, Moacyr
    Max and the cats / Moacyr Scliar.

Translation of: Max e os felinos.
ISBN 0-88619-418-0

    I. Title.

PQ9698.29.C54M3913 2003   869.3   C2003-900486-4

The publisher gratefully acknowledges the support of the Canada Council for
the Arts and the Ontario Arts Council for its publishing program. We acknowledge the support of the Government of Ontario through the Ontario Media
Development Corporation's Ontario Book Initiative.

We acknowledge the financial support of the Government of Canada through
the Book Publishing Industry Development Program (BPIDP) for our publishing activities.

L&OD
an imprint of
Key Porter Books Limited
70 The Esplanade
Toronto, Ontario
Canada M5E 1R2

www.keyporter.com

Printed and bound in Canada

03 04 05 06 07 6 5 4 3 2 1

FOR MY FRIENDS AND FIRST READERS

Lydia

Regina

Isaac

Ivan

Maria da Glória

José Onofre

Maria Helena

• • •

For Klaus and Seldi

CONTENTS

∿∿∿∿∿∿∿∿∿∿∿

Me, afraid?
The tiger fears no one....
The invisible tiger.
My soul.

—FRANCESCO MACIAS NGUEME,
deposed director of
Equatorial Guinea

the
TIGER
on the
WARDROBE

ONE way or another, Max had always been involved with felines.

Born in Berlin in 1912, the son of a furrier, Max grew up amid furs. He particularly liked the fur of the leopard, unfortunately a rare article in his father's store, a small commercial establishment located in a rather disreputable neighborhood of Berlin. It was mostly rejects that found their way to his father's store: foxes of dubious pedigree, dead minks chanced upon in the snow, martens rejected by other furriers. And even rabbits— but this was a taboo subject never brought up at home— stood a chance of being sold there to the more gullible shoppers. There was nothing refined about Hans

Schmidt, neither as a person nor as a merchant. Heavy-set like a bear, he came on too strong when he extolled the qualities of his merchandise: he would holler, turn red, spray the faces of the customers with spittle. And at home, between spoonfuls of soup, slurped noisily, he would boast to his wife and son about the countless suckers he had conned in his life. They would listen to him in silence, Max and his mother. Erna Schmidt was the exact opposite of her husband—a shy, petite woman, she was sensitive, and not entirely lacking in culture. As a teenager, her ambition had been to become an elocutionist; and now, at nights, amid entangled dreams, she would recite poems by Goethe and Schiller in a loud voice. Her husband would roughly shake her awake: I can't sleep, he would yell, because of this folly of yours. Erna never reacted to the brutishness of her husband; sometimes, however, while telling a story to her son, she would suddenly interrupt herself and hug him, bursting into tears.

All of this grieved Max, who had inherited from his mother an almost morbid sensitivity. The furs were a source of both grief and pleasure. Ever since he was a child, he had been in the habit of seeking refuge in the stockroom—not more than a cubbyhole that got some air and light from a tiny window covered with thick iron bars. In that place Max felt happy. He loved to bury his face in the furs, especially if they were from felines (a fact that later turned out to be ironic). At the thought that the fur he was touching had once covered the body of a graceful animal that used to chase gazelles in Africa, Max would quiver with a strange emotion. Merely the booty captured from the animal? Yes. For Max, however, it was as if the beast were actually there—alive.

And there was the tiger, naturally, the one after which the store was named: *The Bengal Tiger*. The animal had been shot by Hans Schmidt himself, during a trip he had made to India with the Hunters' Club. The description of this adventure aroused excitement in the boy Max, of course, but mostly it afflicted him with an almost unbearable uneasiness. India, in his father's coarse, jocular words, was a filthy place, teeming with skeletal natives called the Untouchables. As far as Hans Schmidt was concerned, the only worthwhile aspect of the trip had been the tiger hunt, which he would recount with a profusion of details. He would talk about the impenetrable jungles, about the mysterious night noises, about the tense expectation with which the hunters, perched on platforms mounted in the trees, waited for the tiger. And all of a sudden, the beast coming into sight in the clearing, then the dead shot—his, Hans Schmidt's— and there it was now, stuffed, on the top of the wardrobe. As a matter of fact, the taxidermist had done a superb job. The skin was practically intact, the bullet hole barely visible. The viscera, extracted through the beast's huge mouth, had been replaced with high-quality stuffing material. The eyes, although made of glass, were perfect. In a certain slant of light, they would glint with a fierce brightness, a brightness that Max had never seen in the eyes of the tigers in the zoo, but then, those animals were old, resigned to captivity.

Ever since his early childhood, Max had always been afraid of the tiger. This fear even caused him nightmares. He would wake up in the night screaming, much to the despair of his mother, who, on top of all her other problems, suffered from asthma and was only too familiar with the terrors of the night. Hans Schmidt would scoff at his son's fears, seizing every opportunity to taunt him: A coward, that's what you are, a coward. One evening after dinner he sent the boy to the store to fetch a newspaper that he had presumably left there. Max, nine years old at the time, raised objections—the intense cold, the darkness—but his father, irritated, told him to hurry and stop being so chickenhearted. Bursting into tears, Erna beseeched her husband not to force the child to go out. For heaven's sake, don't do this to him. Max, tense, sat there, watching his parents argue. Suddenly he stood up, and without a word, grabbed his coat and left. He headed for the store.

Max walked hurriedly along the deserted streets. As he turned a corner, he ran into a large crowd of people marching in the middle of the street; they were carrying torches and singing hymns. It was a demonstration held by the socialists. The marchers advanced slowly; one of them signaled to Max to join them.

Then all of a sudden, a clatter of hooves: mounted

policemen, their sabers unsheathed, began charging at the demonstrators. In the melee, Max saw a man fall, his skull cracked open by the blow of a saber. Terrified, he ran to his father's store, which was in the vicinity. He was shaking so badly that he was having a hard time inserting the key into the keyhole; finally, he went in, hid himself behind a mannequin, and there he remained in the dark, his teeth chattering. Gradually, the screams outside subsided. Then silence fell upon the street.

Max kept staring steadily at the tiger. There it was, on the top of the wardrobe, its eyes glinting with a sinister brightness whenever the headlights of a passing car lit up the inside of the store. Between the two of them, between the boy and the beast, was the counter, upon which lay the newspaper. The newspaper that Max would never be able to reach, at least not while paralyzed by a fear the like of which he had never experienced before. A humiliating fear, mingled with a hidden and contained rebellion. Why did his father want this particular newspaper? Did it contain news of such great import that he had to read it? Why—and the tears were streaming down his face—was he so cruel to his son, to his only son?

Then an idea occurred to him: the kiosk around the corner was perhaps still open; what if he were to buy a copy of the newspaper there? But it wouldn't work. Upon opening the store on the following day, Hans Schmidt would find the newspaper lying on the counter; Max wouldn't be able to bear his father's jeering remarks. No. He would have to conquer his fear, confront

the tiger, snatch the paper from the counter, then clear
out of there—and arrive home as if nothing out of the
ordinary had happened. *There you are, Father. Anything
else you want?* But Max, clinging to the mannequin,
seemed rooted to the spot. His legs wouldn't obey him.

The telephone started to ring: his father, very likely,
annoyed at his delay. (*What in the world are you doing
there? Sniffing at the furs, I bet, you sissy.*) Stop ringing,
stop, stop, Max, frightened, kept murmuring, but the
phone rang on persistently, and then, shoving the mannequin aside, he made a dash for the newspaper, but
he stumbled, and crashed against the counter. The glass
shattered and he gashed his hand on the shards. The
sharp pain made him scream, but even so, he picked up
the newspaper, and bleeding profusely, he went home.
On seeing him, his mother started to scream hysteri-
cally. It's nothing, Max said, trying to calm her down.
Then he handed the bloody newspaper to his father.
The bewildered face of that man was the last thing that
Max saw before blacking out.

No, Max didn't like the store—the domain of his father
and of the Bengal tiger. But he did like the stockroom.
Over the years he had gotten into the habit of seeking
refuge there when he wanted to read—which Hans
Schmidt considered odd, but even so, he would humor
his son in this matter—he was, after all, a father. It was
in the stockroom that Max read Andersen and Grimm,
and at his mother's insistence, Goethe and Schiller. But

what he really enjoyed reading were travel narratives, beginning with the ones in a collection entitled *The Adventures of Little Peter*. Thanks to these picturesquely illustrated books, Max got to know, so to speak, Africa (*Kleine Peter geht nach Afrika*), Japan (*Kleine Peter geht nach Japan*), and shunning India, whose image had been duly tarnished by his father, he arrived in Brazil (*Kleine Peter . . . Brazilien*), a country that held a definitive fascination for him. Already on the third or fourth page, there was a picture of Little Peter in the middle of the jungle, looking astonished, but without fear, at a huge feline (a jaguar, according to the text) that had just devoured an aborigine, one of his feet still dangling from the corner of the beast's huge mouth. Notwithstanding this feast, or precisely because of it, the jaguar wore a benevolent, if not good-tempered, look—which was in sharp contrast with the Bengal tiger; for this reason, Max got the impression that Brazil must be a joyful, happy country. One day I'll visit this fascinating place, he wrote in his journal. He was a teenager without friends, and his habit of seeking refuge in the stockroom only furthered his inclination for solitude. In the stockroom he smoked his first cigarette; there he masturbated, and there he was to have sexual intercourse for the first time.

This woman, this Frida, worked in the store as its only employee; given the small volume of business, there was no need for more. She was a rather short, plump girl, cheerful and garrulous. The daugher of peasants from the south, she was far from being a refined person. She would tell Max smutty jokes in coarse language, and on seeing the youth blush, she would split her sides with laughter.

Having to be away one afternoon, Hans Schmidt asked Frida to mind the store during his absence. You can go without worrying, boss, she said, but no sooner had he left than she locked the front door and ran to the stockroom, where Max, as usual, was lying on the furs, reading.

Frida started to try on various coats, parading herself back and forth. What do you think, Max? Doesn't it make me look like a lady? and she would smile and wink at him. Max, perturbed, would look at her askance. She turned the radio on. The chords of a tango inundated the stockroom.

"Come on, let's dance."

Max mumbled something about not knowing how to dance, but she pulled him up toward her. They began to dance, cheek to cheek, and Max, feeling the softness of her skin against his, was becoming more and more aroused. Finally, the two of them tumbled into the furs. Leave it to me, she whispered. She was experienced, everything went off without a hitch. . . . Everything without a hitch. When Hans Schmidt returned, Frida was already back at her post behind the counter, and Max was in the stockroom, his face, still red, hidden behind a book; from the top of the wardrobe, the Bengal tiger stared fixedly at Max, as usual.

On the following day, however, Hans Schmidt fired his employee. Had he suspected something? Perhaps. Whatever the reason, he forbade the girl to ever set foot in the store again; and he warned Max that from then on he was to stay away from her.

But it was impossible for Max to forget that afternoon in the stockroom. . . . He was always daydreaming about the young woman and would write her passionate letters—which he would promptly destroy—until finally, unable to bear it any longer, he went to see her at her house. Frida, all smiles, received him without rancor, as if nothing had happened. She asked after his father, the store, even the tiger. Then, on an impulse, they embraced; they made love on the sofa in the small living room, oblivious to the presence of her aunt, a deaf and blind old woman who was sitting in a rocking chair, intoning old Tyrolean songs. Afterward, as they were arranging themselves, Frida asked in a casual tone if that fox fur coat in the stockroom had been sold yet. Max said that it hadn't.

"In that case," she said, looking at him in a strange way, "next time you want me, come with the coat, or don't bother to come."

Late that night, Max took the key of the store and went there to steal the coat; for once, the Bengal tiger didn't frighten him at all. So that his father wouldn't suspect him of the theft, Max wrenched the bars off the tiny window with a crowbar and then scattered the furs all over the store; as a final gesture—and not without a certain feeling of revenge—he hurled the stuffed tiger on the floor. Although puzzled by the fact that only one coat had been stolen, Hans Schmidt was furious. At the table during lunch, he launched into a harangue before his wife and son; he shouted that there was no honesty in Germany anymore, that the country had become a lair of thieves and left-wingers.

That night Max hurried to take the fur coat to Frida, who was delighted:

"You've done this for me, Max!"

She took him to her bedroom; the lovemaking was quick but fiery. When it was over, she got out of bed naked, put on the coat, and began to parade herself before the mirror, laughing. Max became aroused, wanted to make love again, but suddenly annoyed, she rebuffed him: That's enough! she said, you're asking too much for such a tacky coat. Max felt his cheeks burning; without a word, he put his clothes on and left.

Three days later, on a Saturday, he and his father were walking downtown on their way home when all of a sudden Hans Schmidt stopped short. What's the matter? Max asked, but his father made no reply. *Stop!* he yelled, breaking into a headlong run amid the startled passersby.

He was in hot pursuit of Frida, whom Max recognized by the fur coat.

The chase didn't last long: the woman tripped, and

rolled on the pavement. Hans Schmidt threw himself upon her and began slapping her around:

"You floozy! You thief!"

Frida was defending herself as best she could. Frightened, Max looked on, not knowing whether or not to intervene.

"Help me, Max! Tell him it wasn't me that stole the coat. Do tell him, Max!"

Max rushed up to his father, tried to hold him back, but was unsuccessful—the man was in a rage. By then two policemen were already approaching. They separated Hans and Frida, and after some questioning, they took both of them to the police station. The small crowd that had gathered dispersed amid laughter and facetious remarks. Not knowing what to do, Max went home. His father returned home in the evening, with the fur coat under his arm, but he was outraged. According to him, Frida had been released because of her connections in the police force.

"There's no such thing as honor in this country anymore, Max. Germany has gone astray. This country is rotten, rotten to the core."

He let himself fall upon a chair with such a helpless expression that for the first time, Max felt sorry for him. It wasn't the authoritarian and brutal Hans Schmidt that was sitting there with his head bowed, his shoulders hunched; it was a bewildered and frightened man, an individual worthy of compassion. Max went up to him and put his hand on his father's shoulder. Not knowing exactly what to say, he volunteered to help his father in the store: You don't need that woman, Father, I can work for you. Hans Schmidt raised his head, with the mocking glitter already in his eyes:

"You, a furrier? No way. You're much too refined to get involved in business."

A moment later, however, he took back what he had said. No, son, he went on, melancholy, I don't want you to pursue such a discredited occupation, it's fit only for Jews, really. If I'm in this line of business, it's only because I quit school, and I have no skills.

"But you, Max, you'll go to university," he said, rising to his feet. "I want you to be somebody. A leader, of the kind that Germany needs."

Just as his father had predicted, at the university Max turned out to be a remarkably capable student with multiple interests. When he first began his course of studies, he considered devoting himself to law and the human sciences, but soon his fascination for the exotic led him to the field of the natural sciences. He started to frequent the laboratories of Professor Kunz, famous for his research work on animal psychology—at the time a relatively new specialty. The Professor was then studying the behavior of cats in situations involving conflict. He would place the animals in huge labyrinths, where they were subjected to constant dilemmas, such as choosing between two paths—one leading to a saucer with milk, the other to a fierce bulldog. Such experiments will soon be of great practical value—Kunz, a man who kept a watchful eye on the development of sociopolitical events, would say.

(Much later, when the war was already drawing to an end, the Professor was to expand the field of his experiments, and for this purpose, he would use mostly Gypsies. In one such experiment, young Gypsies, with microphones hanging from their necks, were thrown out of airplanes; the Professor hoped that during the plunge to their deaths, the subjects would supply him with a statement, or if not, with at least a clue—like a scream, primordial or not—that would throw light upon the meaning of existence, which was the Professor's major concern in those days, for with the Allies already at the gates of Berlin, he wanted to learn something about the transition to eternal life. His hopes were frustrated. The Gypsies would smash to the ground with a dull thud but without even one single peep. Headphones on, Kunz would anxiously listen for some manifestation from them—but in vain. Finally, he was compelled to publish the negative results of this study, but he tried to play them down with a complex theory about the relationship between the nomadism of the Gypsies and their silent trajectory toward death. In their covered wagons, stated the Professor at the end of his report, the Gypsies roam across the land in search of annihilation, but they do so in silence, which explains why his research failed. He concluded by suggesting that a different approach be taken in future undertakings of this nature: Hurl *both* gypsies *and* their covered wagons into an abyss.)

Max was rather skeptical about such speculations, but he was fond of the Professor because, among other reasons, Kunz, like Kleine Peter, had traveled in countless exotic countries, gathering specimens for his experiments. He had, for instance, lived in Brazil for a number of years. Max never tired of listening to the Professor's picturesque descriptions of the creatures living in the tropical jungle: the giant butterflies, the quaint sloths, and above all, the mysterious felines. One day I'll have to visit those places, he would sigh. He was nineteen years old then, a thin youth of average height, with an angular face and a defiant expression in his eyes. He was good-natured, and deep down he considered himself an optimist; in this respect he was different from Harald, his classmate and best friend. They were both the same age, they were alike in appearance and even wore the same kind of eyeglasses with gold wire frames, and they saw eye to eye on various issues. Harald, however, was a socialist—like his father, who had, as a matter of fact, taken part in that demonstration Max had seen on the day he had gone to the fur store to get the newspaper for his father. Having narrowly escaped death that night, Harald's father became bitter about political things, and his bitterness rubbed off onto his son. Harald, a believer in the class struggle, had joined a clandestine organization. Rivers of blood must flow before we can pass from the kingdom of necessity to the kingdom of freedom, he would say. Notwithstanding such bombastic statements, he would admit that he was incapable of killing a fly. He hoped that others, braver than he was, would carry out this difficult task, while he would do his best to assist them—perhaps by writing articles. Or poems.

Max, who was seeing Frida again, was feeling great. Deeply appreciative of Max's attempt to rescue her from his father's blows, she was now very sweet to him. They met only once a week, and always on the sly, for she was now married to a man who ran a small business. This man, whom Max knew from photographs, was a Nazi; on Thursday nights (when Frida and Max had their rendezvous) he went to a party meeting, from which he would return drunk and euphoric, announcing that Nazism would soon conquer the world. He wants to dominate the world, Frida would sneer, but in bed he has no lead in his pencil. Max, too, would laugh at the Nazis, who struck him as ridiculous. Harald, however, was becoming alarmed: They're already showing their claws, Max, and nobody gives a damn.

Poor Harald. In those days he cut a sorry figure— unshaven, wild-eyed. What he needs is a good fuck, that's what's wrong with him, said Frida, to whom Max had voiced his concern. Why don't you bring him over? she said with an impish look. Feeling jealous, Max almost took offense at the suggestion but ended up admitting that it would do Harald a great deal of good if he were to have sex with a woman—something he

MAX AND THE CATS

hadn't experienced yet—especially with a kind, fun-loving woman like Frida. He persuaded Harald to call on Frida, but the whole thing turned out to be a flop, with the young man in tears confessing that he was impotent. After this incident, Harald really went downhill. One night Harald's mother, with whom he lived, phoned Max to ask him to come around urgently. Upon arriving there, he found his friend crouching behind an armchair, naked, shouting that the Nazis were going to invade his house.

Frida and Max tried to help him as best they could—Frida with money, and Max by trying to get him psychiatric help, which wasn't easy: what with Harald's father having been a well-known left-winger and with Harald himself sharing his father's reputation, no psychiatrist was willing to risk falling into disfavor with the Nazis. Meanwhile, Harald was growing worse by the day; he refused to eat, and responded to all calls of nature in bed.

One day Max got an anguished phone call from Frida: she had to talk to him, it was a matter of great urgency. I'll be right right there, said Max.

"No, not here. I'll explain later."

They agreed to meet at a small restaurant in the outskirts of the city. Max was the first to arrive; a moment later Frida came in, her face hidden behind a heavy veil. She sat down, downed at one gulp the glass of cognac that Max had offered her, and went straight to the heart of the matter:

"You're in deep shit, Max. You'll have to run away."

"Run away?"

"Run away."

Her husband, having found out about her liaison with Max and Harald, had denounced both of them to the secret police. Despite his illness, Harald had been arrested and was being questioned.

"They're hot on your tail now, Max. You must flee the country."

She had already made all the necessary arrangements: she had gotten in touch with the captain of a freighter, a man they could trust. Max would have to go to Hamburg.

"But when?"

"Today. Right away."

Incredulous, Max stared at her. A fantastic story, it seemed to him. Would he have to flee the country? Just because he was having an affair with Frida? How preposterous! He hadn't committed any crime, let alone a political crime. He could understand that they would want to arrest Harald, and he would try his best to have his friend released (another reason why he should stay in Berlin). But why on earth would they want to arrest him, Max? Why? Frida, however, was so distressed that he decided he would pretend to assent to her plan. Okay, he said. I'll go home and start packing. . . .

"No, don't!" Frida was now frantic. "You can't, Max, they'll catch you."

He tried to reassure her as best he could, telling her not to worry, he knew what he was doing. They left the restaurant separately; she took a taxi, and he a bus. Night had already fallen by the time he came to his street. His mother was waiting for him at the corner. From the expression on her face, he knew right away that what Frida had told him was true: the Nazis were, indeed, after him.

"They're in the house," said his mother, on the verge of sobbing. "They've interrogated your father. . . ."

She burst into tears. Max hugged her. Don't worry, he whispered, it's just a misunderstanding, it'll soon be cleared up, you'll see, all I have to do is to make myself scarce for a while. . . .

She wiped her tears, then looked at him, trying to smile. Go now, she said, and God be with you. Opening her purse, she removed a small pouch made of dark velvet.

"Here's some money for you. And my jewels. They might come in handy."

They kissed. Then Max turned around and hurried away. He glanced back only once and his mother was still standing there, motionless, in the light fog. That was the last time that he was to see her.

From a public telephone he called Frida to ask for further information about the ship, the voyage. She explained everything in detail and reassured him. As I've already told you, you can trust the captain, who's actually a relative of mine. In two or three weeks you'll be landing at the port of Santos, in Brazil.

· · ·

It was only at that moment that Max realized that he had never asked about his destination. Brazil? The exotic country? At first the idea filled him with an almost childish enthusiasm; a moment later, he was on the brink of panic. Brazil? What did he know about this place—Brazil? Hardly anything at all: only what he had picked up by reading the *Kleine Peter* books. And by listening to Professor Kunz's narratives. In fact, he had many unanswered questions. Questions about . . . the natives, for instance. Their physical aspect. Their build: tall, short, well fed, undernourished? The color and texture of their hair. The color of their eyes. The shape of their skulls. The condition of their teeth. Their habits: peculiar or not. Their ancestry: Caucasian, Mongolian, other? Their language. Their traditions. Was there a god they worshiped in particular? With what kind of rituals? What was the current attitude toward human sacrifice? As for their temperament—were they gentle? Loquacious, reserved? Obliging, defiant? Tolerant of foreigners?

Questions about their form of government. Their coat of arms (a brief description would suffice). Their national anthem. Their flag. Questions about agricultural output. Coastal navigation and trade. Mining. Air, land, river, lake transportation. Currency.

Questions about the climate. Dry, rainy? Were trade winds present or not? The relative humidity of the atmosphere. How would he like an air so heavily saturated with moisture that it would make breathing difficult and cause clothes and papers to disintegrate?

Questions—notwithstanding Kunz's narratives—about the fauna and flora. Were they true, those rumors about the presence of large carnivorous plants? Types of orchids. Felines. *Felines.*

"Hello! Hello! Max, can you hear me?" It was Frida, impatient. "Answer me, Max."

"Yes," said Max, "I can hear you."

"Thank goodness," she replied, "I thought we had been disconnected."

She was now bidding him farewell, she couldn't talk any longer; she wished him luck, and would pray to God that one day . . .

Farewell, said Max. He hung up the phone and made for the railroad station, where he took the train to Hamburg.

Disquieting news awaited him at the docks in Hamburg: the *Schiller*, the ship that was supposed to take him to Brazil, had just sailed. Someone suggested another freighter, also headed for the same destination. Max went to see the Captain.

A rather sinister type, this captain. He had a long black beard, and like the pirates of bygone days, he wore an eye patch. Suspiciously, he fixed his gaze on Max.

Yes, he was sailing for the port of Santos. No, he didn't take passengers on.

But Max persisted, offering to give him half of his money, and then the whole amount. The Captain finally gave in.

"But listen carefully," he said. "I won't take any responsibility for whatever happens to you, is that clear?"

Max thought that the warning was nothing but a formality; he couldn't predict what was in store for him. . . . Max said it was all right by him, he was all set to go, come what may. The Captain then took him on board the ship, and showed him to a narrow, stuffy cabin.

"It's the best we've got."

Max said it was fine. The *Germania* weighed anchor that very night. From the quarterdeck Max watched the city lights disappear in the distance. The die was cast.

The first few days aboard the ship were hard on Max. The food was awful, he was seasick, and at night, what with the din made by the engines and some mysterious noises—howls and shrieks—he couldn't sleep. It was all very strange, but then there were plenty of other weird things going on aboard the ship—the crew, for instance, steered clear of him—but then Max was not in a position to ask questions, much less to complain. Anyhow, gradually he got used to life on board.

Despite what the Captain had told him, Max wasn't the only passenger. There was another one, a middle-aged Italian, a pleasant, cheerful man who paraded the deck as if he were strolling along a boulevard in a big city: always wearing a suit and a tie, and carrying a silver-topped cane. He spoke bad German, this Signor Ettore, but even so Max began to seek him out after learning that the man had lived in Brazil. He told Max that he was returning to that country after a tour of Europe. He was the managing director of a zoo or some kind of a circus. The animals were in the hold of the ship (which explained the howls and shrieks that Max heard at night). As a matter of fact, the news about animals on board left Max apprehensive. Mustering courage, he talked to the Captain about this matter. The man laughed. A danger? If there's anyone exposed to danger, it's the poor beasts in the hands of—and he pointed to the sailors—those animals over there.

Signor Ettore was enthusiastic about Brazil. One can make a lot of money there, he would assure Max. Not in my case, though, he would hasten to add, but then it was only because (breaking into a roguish smile) I've always enjoyed all the good things in life: women, gambling, booze.

Despite all the friendliness of the Italian, Max didn't feel entirely at ease with him. It seemed to him that Signor Ettore was hiding something, that there was more to this voyage than met the eye—an impression reinforced by the fact that on two or three different occasions, he had seen the Italian talking in hushed tones to the Captain. Max, however, was determined not to get involved in any imbroglio; he already had enough problems of his own. All he wanted was to arrive in Brazil, where he would stay for a year or two—until the Nazis were cast down from power—and then return to Germany, back to a normal life, living with his parents, and attending the university. He pictured the day when he would tell his friends about the voyage in the *Germania*; he wished that his present situation were already a thing of the past. At the thought of his parents, tears would well up in his eyes. Instead of keeping a journal, he took to writing long, mournful letters (would he ever be able to mail them?), and in this way time seemed to go by faster, and the separation from his family was less painful. He even missed the tiger on the top of the wardrobe, and if he was still hopeful that he would see it again one day, it was because he had no way of foretelling the future.

One night Max woke up with the feeling that something was amiss on board the ship. The animals were more agitated than usual. He sat up in bed. Yes, something strange was going on: he could hear the sounds of hurried footsteps, of a vague clamor. Throwing on his clothes, he left his cabin—and at that very moment the lights went out. In the semidarkness he could see indistinct shapes running to and fro. What's going on? he asked, but got no reply. He made for the upper deck—and only then did he notice that the ship was listing, and that it continued to list increasingly faster. Captain! he shouted. Signor Ettore! He got no reply; the sailors were busy lowering the lifeboats. Only then did it dawn on Max: the ship was sinking. The lifeboats were quickly lowered, and soon there was nobody on board. Frightened, he made a dash for the gunwale.

"Don't leave me behind!"

In vain: the boats were moving away fast. Ah, you traitors, shouted Max. Suddenly, he got it: the *Germania* was never meant to arrive at its destination, the shipwreck had been planned all along. Now things began to fall into place—the strange behavior of the Captain and the Italian, their furtive talks. What they undoubtedly had in mind was to collect the insurance taken out on the old ship and also on the animals. To boot, the Captain must have decided to keep Max's money as well. He certainly didn't expect Max to survive to tell the tale. You crooks, he snarled, but he shouldn't be wasting any more time, the *Germania* would sink any minute now. He made a dash for the stern and there—what a miracle!—he found a dinghy. With great difficulty he managed to lower it to the sea. Then, groping about in the dark, he found an oar. He knew that a sinking ship created a whirpool strong enough to suck small vessels down into the abyss; therefore, he started paddling, and he paddled away with might and main.

At first light, Max found himself alone in the vastness of the ocean. Seized by intense anxiety, he burst into tears, and cried his eyes out. What a dismal predicament. What a dismal life. A childhood that hadn't been exactly happy; a tortured adolescence; the hurried flight from his homeland; and on top of everything else, this shipwreck. It was all too much. He was crying, yes, crying and also berating himself: Why in the world did he ever get mixed up with a married woman? With a left-wing crackpot? Didn't he know then that things were bound to come to a bad end?

Max cried for a long time. Finally, he wiped his tears and looked about him, resigned. Tears wouldn't be of any help. He would have to take stock of the situation and decide what to do next.

The sea, smooth—in fact as smooth as a mirror—was full of the debris of the shipwreck, but since there were no ships in sight, he might as well forget about rescue being close at hand; later on, maybe, or on the following days. As for the dinghy, it was solid and well equipped for emergencies: in a large oilcloth bag Max found canned foods, containers filled with water, fishing tackle, a flashlight. Which reinforced his initial suspicions—nothing but a plot, this shipwreck—but also rekindled his hopes. He now had the means to survive, all he had to do was to wait for a passing ship to pick him up.

Max was wrong again in supposing that lack of food was the greatest danger he would be facing as the survivor of a shipwreck. There was the sun.

By the afternoon of the second day he was already suffering from severe sunburn. He felt dizzy, he had a headache; with alarm, he realized that he was suffering hallucinations. On the horizon, he saw mountains, which dissolved when he rubbed his eyes; he saw bicyclists in white uniforms riding among the waves. And suddenly Harald was sitting in front of him. Harald! he cried out. What a surprise, Harald! So you've managed to escape, my friend! And you were on the same ship, too! But I had no idea that you were on board! To each of these exclamations Harald responded only with a doleful smile.

"Are you sore at me, Harald? Is it that you think I deserted you? I didn't, Harald. It's just that I had to flee in a hurry. I couldn't even take leave of my father, and to my mother, I only said a hasty good-bye. And God only knows when I'll see them again, Harald . . . Come on now, Harald, there's no reason why you should be mad at me."

Harald, silent, with a fixed smile, the wind ruffling his hair.

"Why don't you say something, Harald? Come on, man, talk to me. We have to discuss our situation . . . devise a plan. Our survival is at stake. Speak, Harald! Say something!"

Harald, motionless. Then all of a sudden the wind carried away his hair, exposing a bald pate; and a moment later his skin began to peel off, reducing his face to a grinning skull. Letting out a howl, Max extended his hand to his friend, but at that moment the vision dissolved and he found himself alone again in the dinghy. It had been another hallucination; again, produced by the sun. He would have to protect himself, but how? There was nothing in the dinghy that could be used as a shelter.

Then he had an idea. He would improvise some kind

of a hut with the wreckage of the *Germania* that was floating around him. A big wooden box drifting along seemed suitable for this purpose. With great effort, he began to row toward it.

Max pulled the box toward the boat. Upon examining it, he saw that there was a lid on the top fastened with a padlock, now broken and hanging loose. He removed the padlock.

Something leaped out of the box, throwing him with unprecedented force to the bottom of the dinghy. Max hit his head, and blacked out.

Gradually he came to. He opened his eyes.

The howl that he let out resounded in the air. In front of him, seated on the bench of the dinghy, was a jaguar.

the
JAGUAR
in the
DINGHY

OH, God, help me. Jesus Christ, have pity on me. Father, Mother, come to my rescue. Please, help me. . . .
His eyes closed, his hands gripping the edges of the dinghy, his body shaken by violent tremors, Max waited for the end, which would come, first, with a tremendous blow delivered by the huge paw; immediately afterward, the beast would pounce on him, drive its fangs into his belly, his arms, his thighs, tearing away chunks of muscle, crushing his bones, and he suffering death amid racking pains . . . *Lord, to thee I commend my soul.*

However, nothing happened. Seconds or hours went by, and nothing happened. Slowly, still terrified, Max opened his eyes.

The jaguar was still there, motionless, his eyes fixed on him.

What a huge feline. Perhaps not as big as the stuffed tiger in his father's store, but nevertheless, quite big. The coloring was different: this one was reddish yellow with black spots. Initially, Max had confused him with a tiger, but now he was able to identify the feline: It was indeed a jaguar (*Panthera jaguarius*); however, he drew no solace from this fact, and how could he, faced as he was with the most frightful beast of the Americas (*Kleine Peter*; Kunz). Max was at a loss to explain why the jaguar hadn't devoured him yet; by then, nothing should have remained of him. A few bloody bones, perhaps. A foot. Fragments of scalp.

For the time being, however, it seemed that the jaguar didn't feel like attacking. The beast remained motionless and calm, and there was even an air of ennui about him.

Why, Max didn't know. He didn't know much about the habits of a feline; and even if he were an expert in this field, under the circumstances he simply wouldn't be able to think straight. Maybe the jaguar wasn't hungry at that moment; maybe he had been fed before the shipwreck (what for, if he was doomed to die?). Maybe he felt insecure, there in that flimsy dinghy; maybe he was afraid of the sea, so different from his usual habitat. Maybe he felt grateful to Max, his savior (albeit a reluctant one); maybe he was a domesticated jaguar, a dependent, submissive animal with a fondness for man. Or maybe he was a sly beast feigning calmness, waiting for the opportune moment to attack.

Max relaxed somewhat. Death no longer seemed so imminent; he would bide his time, come up with something. What if he were to jump into the sea and swim to the floating box, thus changing places with the feline? Obviously, he would then forfeit everything that was in the dinghy, all the means of survival; but on the other hand, he would have a chance to escape. Out of the corner of his eye, he looked at the box, assessing the distance: not too far away, twenty meters or so. How would the jaguar react if Max were suddenly to get up and plunge into the water? He would spring at him, undoubtedly, but would he succeed in catching him? While still in the dinghy? In midair? Would the jaguar pursue him in the sea? And who would be the better swimmer? Max, who had won a medal in school (one hundred meters, breaststroke, in the category of children), or the feline, a member of a species widely known for its aversion to water? Useless guesswork. At that moment the wind picked up, the box oscillated, filled with water, and sank.

Max then realized that he was wet. He had pissed his pants. Out of fear. Something that had never happened to him before, not even as a child in situations of the utmost panic. How very humiliating! Max shed a few more tears, the jaguar watching him.

The sun was beginning to set, and the two of them were still eyeball to eyeball. Frozen still. Max was uncomfortable, his back hurt, but he didn't dare to stir. He could only hope that a ship would appear and rescue him—but he wouldn't even risk looking about him; any inattention on his part, and the beast might pounce upon him. At one point he even thought that a ship in sight would only make matters worse, for unless they succeeded in killing the animal at long range—a dead shot, like the one fired by Hans Schmidt—Max would be the first to suffer the consequences, should the jaguar feel cornered. A ship? No. Better not.

The jaguar let out a roar.

Well, it wasn't exactly a roar, more like a hoarse meow, but strong enough to startle Max, who almost fell into the sea. He had barely recovered himself before he was startled anew: the animal growled, opening its large mouth wide. The glimpse of the huge fangs and of the red fauces did nothing to reassure poor Max. The jaguar wanted something, there was no doubt about it, but what was it?

Food, of course.

What else could the jaguar possibly want? Without having eaten anything for hours, he must be starving. It fell to Max (who else was there?) to feed him. But how? And what?

Another growl. Max would have to act fast.

Gingerly—lest the beast should misinterpret his gesture—he reached for the oilcloth bag, took out a cracker, and placed it on the floor in front of the jaguar. The feline merely sniffed at the cracker, without even deigning to touch it. Not his kind of food, concluded Max, breaking into a cold sweat. Of course, carnivores eat meat, not crackers. But where in the world would Max get hold of meat? Of fresh meat, dripping with blood, more to the liking of a fierce jaguar?

Without averting his eyes from the beast, Max picked up a fishing line (luckily, there was already bait on the hook) and cast it into the sea, praying that a fish would soon nibble at the bait. He was in luck: before long, he caught a medium-sized fish. With trepidation—how would his new offering be received?—he laid it before the jaguar.

The feline sniffed at the fish, still moving, in the throes of death. With one stroke of his paw—what a hair-raising scene—the jaguar killed it, tore it to pieces with his claws, then devoured the bloody chunks (Max cherishing a fleeting hope: he will choke on it, he will suffocate to death; soon replaced by fear: but he might kill me before he dies; followed by some kind of relief: the jaguar had apparently relished the fish, which could represent some protection to a person who, like Max, had always regarded himself as a mediocre fisherman, unable to survive if his subsistence were to depend on fishing, this age-old occupation).

In quick succession—was it possible that he was in the midst of a shoal of migrating fish?—Max took fish after fish out of the sea: a veritable prodigy, a biblical miracle. But just as quickly the jaguar kept devouring them.

Suddenly Max was hungry. Really hungry. His appetite had been whetted by the sight of the jaguar eating the fish; he now realized that he, too, hadn't eaten for some time. There were the crackers and some other foodstuff—but what he felt was a craving, an absurd craving for *fish*. For the fish that he, Max, had caught. Even uncooked, he wanted his fish. Even just one tiny piece would do.

The jaguar now seemed satiated; and there were still three fish, small ones, on the bottom of the boat. What if he were to . . . ?

Slowly, Max began to extend his hand.

Impassive, the jaguar kept staring at him.

Max's fingers would advance a few millimeters, then stop; a few more millimeters, then stop again. He was now on the verge of reaching the fish.

All of a sudden the jaguar covered the fish with his paw. Seized with fright, Max even fell on his back. He pulled himself together, then panting, he remained there, staring wide-eyed at the jaguar. I'm sorry, he kept murmuring, I'm sorry, I didn't mean to.

Suddenly he came to his senses. What was he doing? Apologizing? What's the use of apologizing to an animal? Besides—why should he apologize? After all, he had caught the fish, hadn't he? No, no apologies. He was entitled to those fish. If not to all of them, at least to half. He'd be content with two; one, even. Sure, he was entitled to something.

Gnawing at the hard cracker that the jaguar had spurned, Max stood looking at him—not with fear, though, but with resentment, hatred even. A carnivore, all right; but why so unfair? Why so rude?

·   ·   ·

Night fell, a dark, moonless night it was. Max could barely discern the shadowy form of the jaguar. Had he fallen asleep? Maybe; he had, after all, eaten well. And if he were asleep, would it be possible to . . . ? No, Max wasn't plotting anything; however, he would have to find out about the beast's sleeping habits and study them carefully for future reference; such knowledge could come in handy. And if he still hadn't devised any plans, he could mull over this matter during the long night (nights?) ahead of him.

Moving with infinite caution, Max picked up the flashlight.

Still hesitating for a moment—God's will be done— he switched it on. The beam of light flashed in the darkness—the eyes of the jaguar, glittering, were fixed on him. Max shuddered, switched the flashlight off, and put it away.

Now he knew. The jaguar didn't sleep. He never would. Max couldn't count on the animal's sleep in order to make an escape. Besides, how would he escape? Where to?

A deep depression, an overpowering sadness, took hold of Max. Again, he carried his thoughts back to his father, his mother, the comfort of his bed in Berlin; he felt a strong urge to cry, but he didn't cry. Curling himself up in the bottom of the boat, he began to hum a song to himself softly—a lullaby that his mother used to sing to him: *Guten Abend, Guten Nacht, Mit Rosen be-*

dacht. No, it wasn't going to be a good night, and he wasn't covered with roses. But even so, he finally drifted off to sleep.

He woke up startled. For a moment he didn't know where he was; soon, however, everything came back to him: the shipwreck, the jaguar . . . And lo and behold, there he was, the feline, staring at him. An evil animal— thought Max. A cruel animal. A horrid animal.

No, not horrid. Beautiful, this jaguar. Magnificent, this shadowy figure silhouetted against the sky, which was beginning to grow light. A ruthless executioner? You bet. But then it was nature that had equipped him so well for this role.

With a sigh, Max sat down on the bench. Scratching his head, he looked at the calm sea. It was going to be beautiful, this day. An ideal day to go for a sail in a yacht . . .

A growl from the jaguar brought him back to reality. He was startled, but not overly so. He now knew what he had to do. He threw the fishhook into the sea; just as on the day before, he was in luck, and caught several fish right away. With a spiritless gaze, he watched the feline devour the fish, wondering if this was to be his lifelong routine: to fish for a jaguar, to feed the beast. What a gloomy forecast for someone who had once gone to college! How much longer would he have to bear such an absurd servitude?

The jaguar stopped eating and lifted his head, growling softly, his ears pricked. Surprised and alarmed, Max looked at him. The animal must have sensed peril. But what kind of peril could it be, in that deserted immensity?

Max soon found out. About one hundred meters from the dinghy, a triangular fin, emerging from the surface of the sea, began moving swiftly in circles.

A shark.

Undoubtedly attracted by the smell of the blood from the fish. But would the shark dare to attack the small boat? Even when on board was an equally, if not more, bloodthirsty beast? Trembling, Max hoped it wouldn't; and, paradoxically, the presence of the feline was a comfort to him, poor shipwrecked person that he was. The jaguar was a known peril, one he could live with, at least while his luck in fishing held; however, if the shark succeeded in capsizing the flimsy vessel, he would be lost. Max hoped against hope that the jaguar, his ruthless tormentor, would protect him. He slid to the bottom of the dinghy, and there he sat, peering in dread over the gunwale.

The shark continued to navigate in circles. It drew closer and closer, with Max and the jaguar following its movements. Suddenly the shark charged. It came swiftly toward the dinghy and crashed into it. The frightful jolt made Max scream out in terror; and a moment later, the huge, ugly head emerged right next to the edge of the boat, only to receive a powerful, crushing blow of the jaguar's paw. The shark lunged out again, the jaguar delivered another blow—and the boat, rocking violently, threatened to capsize at any moment. Not realizing what he was doing, Max clung to the jaguar, trying to restrain him; but at that moment the shark began to swim away, leaving a trail of blood in the water. A while later, everything calmed down.

Max, shaking, was still hugging the jaguar. Then he became aware of the beast's coarse whiskers against his face, of his acrid breath. What am I doing? he murmured, horrified. What in the world am I doing?

Slowly Max loosened the embrace and returned to his bench. The jaguar, after gazing at him for a moment, calmly went back to his interrupted meal. Max closed his eyes.

(A sudden recollection. They were at the table—his father, his mother, and he, a four-year-old boy then. The maid came in with a plate of meat. His father cut a large piece for himself and began to chew noisily. All of a sudden, he stopped. What's wrong, Hans? his wife asked. He didn't answer—his face red, apoplectic. What's wrong? she persisted, alarmed. He leaped to his feet, overturning the table, which made little Max scream out in fear.

"I've already told you," his father bellowed, "I don't want any cumin in my meat! I don't want any cumin, do you hear me?"

His wife tried to calm him down, he gave her a violent shove, and she fell, hauling him down in the fall. Max ran to his father—and when he realized what he was doing, he was squeezing his father's neck with all the strength of his puny arms. "Hey, do you want to kill me?" asked his father, surprised, and then he burst into laughter. His mother, still fallen on the floor, joined in the laughter. Soon the maid was laughing, too, and everybody was laughing, only Max was crying and crying. Why are you crying, Max? the maid, almost choking with laughter, kept asking, but Max wouldn't reply, and even if he were to reply she wouldn't hear, collapsed on a chair and doubled up in laughter as she was.)

And if all of this were nothing but a dream? And if the jaguar were nothing but a nightmare? The jaguar and the shipwreck? The jaguar, the shipwreck, and the flight from Germany? All of this nothing but a nightmare of the young man Max? Or perhaps even an unusually long and painful nightmare of the boy Max, finally asleep after a day packed with intense emotions (father overturning the table, etc.)?

A light fog was now enveloping them, and in it the jaguar was a shadowy figure of indistinct contours—he could well be a figure in a dream.

As if guessing at Max's thoughts, the feline growled. A figure in a nightmare? Perhaps. But with a ravenous hunger. Sighing, Max began to fish.

Well, perhaps not a dream then, Max thought on the following day; quite possibly, however, he was being the victim of some trick or simulation. What particularly attracted his attention was the mechanical repetition in the beast's routine: he growled, he was given some fish; he growled again, he was given some more. Even the beast's reaction to new situations—like when Max tried to get a fish for himself, or when the shark attacked— amounted to stereotyped blows delivered with a paw. As if the jaguar were an automaton.

Was the jaguar an automaton? A robot-jaguar? The idea wasn't entirely absurd. Max was familiar with those mechanical toys of Nuremberg that imitated live animals perfectly. What's more: it was possible that this jaguar was run by remote control, which would explain even better the fight against the shark, not to mention his jumping out of the box into the dinghy. But from where was this robot being controlled? Perhaps from a submarine. Through a periscope invisible to Max, an eye was probably watching him at this very moment, registering his reactions as he faced the pseudo-jaguar. But whose eye was it? Who was subjecting him to such an ordeal? The Nazis? But for what purpose? Of driving him crazy? Of killing him? Nonsense; if such was their intention, they would have bumped him off already. But what if this whole thing were an experiment, like one of those carried out by Professor Kunz in his laboratory? Yes: a young man, cultured and sensitive, is subjected to a series of traumatic events—first, a fabricated story to force him to flee the country, then the simulated shipwreck, the sharing of a dinghy with what is seemingly a fierce jaguar—how will this man react? So, here it is, the objective of this experiment—gruesome and yet undoubtedly interesting (one that would certainly have fascinated Max, the student). Perhaps concealed under the skin of the false jaguar were devices to observe and record—the eyes being the lenses of movie cameras; the ears, microphones, and so on.

The possibility that he was being used, albeit for scientific purposes, infuriated Max. Looking straight at the jaguar, and not giving a damn about which microphones would pick up his outburst, he shouted:

"You can torture me to death, Professor! I'll never disclose information on the meaning of life!"

The jaguar looked at Max with such genuine astonishment that he was now convinced. No, he wasn't a robot. But he could well be a jaguar that had been trained and conditioned to wander about in the complex labyrinth of his emotions; to serve him as a sparring partner in this struggle for survival; to maltreat but not to kill him; to drive him to exasperation, to the last of his psychic reserves. An experiment possibly set up by Kunz himself. Or by the Brazilian government in connivance with the shipping companies in order to test the sangfroid of immigrants from various countries.

The sun was beginning to set. Have I done anything useful today?—such was the question that children should ask themselves at dusk, according to the boy Max's schoolteacher. Have I helped anyone? Have I cleaned or polished or fixed or improved anything? Have I expressed my gratitude to someone? Have I greeted a neighbor with a smile? Have I helped a little old lady across the street? Have I gently stroked the back of a kitten?

No, the jaguar didn't look like a trained beast. In the magic light of that twilight at sea, he didn't look like a beast at all. He looked like a cat, an oversized cat, true, but with a sad, helpless air about him. Max even pitied this big tom. Maybe I could tame him, he thought. And why not? Wasn't the fact that the feline hadn't devoured him an indication of a secret desire to be subjugated, of a tacit recognition of the supremacy of the human being—the king (albeit weak) of creation, the lord (albeit temporarily and understandably upset by tragic events) of the land and the sea, and above all, of the dinghy, built thanks to the inventiveness and craft of his fellow human beings? After all, this was an animal that had been brought into captivity; that had been whipped into shape; that was used to obeying in order to get food— and considering the fact that he was already getting food, he should, at least in theory, be willing to obey. *As a submissive animal,* Max was thinking, *you'd be a great help to me, my dear fellow. For starters, you could use your paws as paddles, and your instinct as a compass, and thus we could reach land and arrive in this Brazil, which I no longer even know if in fact it exists.*

And once there in Brazil, with the jaguar he would be able to project an impressive image of power. No native would be able to resist a man with a jaguar on the leash. Any undertaking he might venture on—a trading post in the jungle, a rubber plantation, a diamond mine—would be a sure thing.

It was growing dark fast. If he intended to start taming the beast, he would have to get down to work right away. He rose to his feet, and with his eyes always on the feline, he removed his belt and cracked it in the air.

"Attention, cat! Attention!"

The jaguar bared his teeth and growled.

Max began to shake. He was again quaking with fear. Unable to keep a grip on himself, this king of creation (*you rascal! you coward!*), this lord of the land and the sea (*you despicable worm!*) was shaking so badly that the dinghy began to rock; it wasn't on the verge of capsizing, but it was rocking. He had to sit down. Relax, big tom, he whispered, staring wide-eyed at the feline. Relax, everything's okay.

He picked up the fishhooks. There was still sufficient light to fish by, and perhaps catch a small fish or two.

That night he still caught something, but on the following day, his luck, until then on his side, deserted him. He couldn't catch a thing, not even one pitiful sardine. The jaguar was displaying growing impatience. Max opened the canned food that he had been saving for emergencies. Surprisingly, the feline accepted the sausages and even the crackers. He ate with such voracity that Max's heart sank. At this rate, the food supply would soon be exhausted. What was he going to do then?

Two days later there was already nothing to eat. And

Max had been unable to catch anything. Dizzy and feeble, he looked at the jaguar.

"That's it, you devil. We're out of food."

He was. But not the jaguar . . .

Max was so weak that he couldn't think, never mind defend himself. If the jaguar intended to devour him, why didn't he get it over with soon, thus putting an end to his agony? Nothing else mattered to him now. He lay down on the bottom of the boat and didn't even commend his soul to God: he fell into a heavy sleep, the soundest sleep he had had in weeks.

He dreamed that he was a little boy again, and that he was at home, in Berlin. Lying on his parents' bed, he was waiting for the return of his mother, who had gone shopping; he knew she would bring him a present, and in fact, she came back with a big plush cat. He squeezed it—and the cat emitted not a meow but a strange squeal. Although disappointed, Max laughed: a squealing cat, how about that? And then his mother began to squeal and she squealed repeatedly, while he grew increasingly more nervous until he finally woke up.

He woke up, but the squealing continued. With difficulty, he sat up—he paid no attention to the jaguar; it was as if the feline didn't exist—and, dazzled by the brightness, looked around him.

A sea gull, squealing, was wheeling over the boat.

A sea gull—but this was a sign of land! So, the coast couldn't be far away. And if this solitary and graceful sea gull had come from the shore, it would certainly fly back there as soon as it realized that this boat, unlike others, had no food to offer. And when the sea gull set out on its return flight, all he had to do was to follow it. Gathering what little strength he had, Max took hold of the paddle.

"Go, beautiful sea gull!" he shouted in a voice so hoarse that it even startled him. "Go back to your country, sea gull! To Brazil, let's go!"

The sea gull, however, seemed in no hurry to fly back to the shore. Squealing playfully, it continued to wheel over the dinghy. Finally, it came to rest on the edge of the boat, right next to the jaguar.

The feline kept staring at the bird. Max could foretell what was going to happen—but before he could shout, Flee, sea gull, flee from this killer, the jaguar struck, and presto, there was no cheerful sea gull anymore, just a bloody mass that the jaguar proceeded to devour. Oh God, Max moaned. He had reached the limit of his endurance. He couldn't bear this situation any longer; he would have to put an end to it right away. Even at the cost of his own life.

Holding the paddle in his twitching hands, he rose to his feet. *Not one minute more!* The jaguar raised his head.

"I'll kill you, you demon!"

He hurled himself at the jaguar at the very moment when the feline pounced on him. The two of them collided in midair—and Max blacked out.

·   ·   ·

He opened his eyes. Faces were tilted downward; the faces of strangers—mestizos, blacks, some whites, too. They were all looking at him curiously and talking among themselves in a language that he didn't know, but he guessed it to be Portuguese. Brazilians, they were. Whites, mulattoes, blacks, mestizos . . . The Brazilians! Max was safe, aboard a Brazilian ship.

He tried to lift himself up, but they wouldn't let him. A blond sailor stepped forward and addressed him in German.

"Feeling better?"

With a nod of his head Max replied in the affirmative. Where am I? he asked. On a ship, off the Brazilian coast, said the man, who then added with a smile: That was a pretty narrow escape, *mein Freund*. He told Max how they had found him: half-drowned, holding on precariously to a capsized dinghy. Max sat up, his eyes bulging from their sockets:

"And the jaguar? Where's the jaguar?"

They restrained him and made him lie down again. The sailor said something to his companions. Max guessed what he was saying: *He's delirious, he's raving, it must be from thirst, from all that sun.* They brought him water. He drank it eagerly, choking and spluttering. *Mais?* they kept asking him in Portuguese, and he, inferring that the word must mean *more* (it's not so difficult!), kept saying *mais, mais,* delighted with his first word in a new language, delighted with the Brazilian water, delighted with the Brazilians around him. Already, he was no longer thinking of the jaguar.

The following days flowed into one another, filled
with a pleasant routine. First in the ship's small sick-
room and later reclining on a chaise longue on the upper
deck, Max did nothing but rest and eat, following the
fatherly instructions of the captain who, like the rest of
the crew, was especially attentive to the needs of *his*
shipwrecked man. By the time the ship arrived at its
final destination—the city of Porto Alegre—Max was
fully recovered. You'll be able to start a new life here,
said the ship's cook, a fat man from the northern state
of Bahia.

A new life, well, it wasn't going to be easy, Max
thought as he looked at the city skyline before he dis-
embarked. He had already taken a step (a small one, for
sure) in the right direction by selling his gold wristwatch
to the captain in order to raise enough money to see him
through his first few weeks in Porto Alegre (he still had
his mother's jewels, which throughout that time he had
carried in a small pouch hanging from his neck). And
the captain had recommended a boardinghouse run by
a German lady where he would be able to make himself
understood until he learned enough Portuguese. For the
time being, everything was settled. Afterward, everything would be in God's hands.

Max liked Porto Alegre, which reminded him of a European city, especially the district where he lived—Floresta, with its pastry shops and quaint little stores. It is
true that later he discovered the beggars and the slums

in the district of Partenon, but even so, this discovery wasn't enough to tarnish the image he had of the city. In particular, he liked the view that unfolded from his window. The boardinghouse was located on an elevated place, and so he could see the tiled roofs of the bungalows of Floresta; if he were a prying person, he could easily watch the residents of the neighborhood through their open windows. But he had no desire to snoop on anyone; he didn't want to get involved in complications. He looked only at the tiled roofs, at the cats dozing off in the sun; and if his gaze lingered upon a child playing in a backyard, it was perhaps because of a natural fondness that he had for children, a feeling that he didn't want to stifle inside him.

Initially, he hardly ever left his room, which was, as a matter of fact, quite pleasant: large, clean, sunny. He started to keep a journal again, beginning with the episode about the jaguar, the details of which he could recall only with increasing difficulty (almost making him wonder if the whole incident had been nothing but delirium).

Gradually he started to venture out of his refuge, beginning with walks in his neighborhood; later, he set out to familiarize himself with the entire city. He found out that the streetcar shelters, the chalet in Praça Quinze, the Public Market, the Galeria Chaves were interesting places, frequented by a cross section of the population of Porto Alegre. He would board a streetcar, get off at the end of the line, and wander about the outlying districts of Glória, Menino Deus, Partenon.

Wanting to learn Portuguese as soon as possible, he began taking lessons from his landlady's daughter, Elizabeth, a shy, blond girl with a dreamy air about her. Her presence flustered Max, all the more so because he sensed that she, too, became flustered when they were together. If their knees happened to touch under the table, they would blush and laugh to hide their embarrassment. Afterward, they would break into laughter again, a nervous little laugh it was; and then they would remain silent for a while; and then they would sigh; and finally, they would return to the text in front of them— a novel by José de Alencar, a nineteenth-century writer known for his idealized portraits of Indians. Does she like me? Max would wonder. Would something between us be possible?

He had no answer to these, and other questions. In fact, it was difficult for him to think of anything except his own painful past. At the thought of his parents, he would often cry. He would like to write to them, to let them know that everyting was fine, notwithstanding his hasty flight; that he was living in a country where people were friendly, and that he was happy, or almost so. However, he didn't dare to send them a letter, for fear that it might get his parents into trouble; from what he gathered from his reading of the newspapers, the Nazi regime was becoming increasingly more entrenched, more arrogant, more intolerant of opponents, whether real or imagined. He never broached this subject with his landlady or her daughter; he had no idea what their opinions were, and he didn't want to create an embarrassing situation. Besides, he had far more pressing problems: the money from the sale of his wristwatch was already gone, despite the simple life that he led. He couldn't find a job: he barely spoke the language of the country, and what was worse, he had no skills. At one time he got a job in a flower shop, but the owner, who wanted someone more experienced and diligent, ended up firing him. Finally, Max began to contemplate selling his mother's jewels, which he always carried in the small pouch hanging from his neck. It was with great reluctance that he reached the painful decision of selling them; in fact, he had been hoping that one day, amid kisses and tears of joy, he would be able to return them to his mother. But he had already fallen behind on the rent and on the payment of his language lessons as well, and his situation had become increasingly more distressing. Then he saw a small advertisement in the *Correio do Povo*: "We buy jewelry, gold, antiques." He went to the address given.

It was a mansion near Rua Voluntarios da Patria, a building with such a sinister aspect that Max, beginning to have second thoughts about it, was on the point of returning home. However, he couldn't postpone dealing with his financial problem any longer; so, mustering up his courage, he knocked on the door. An old man wrapped in a long black overcoat opened the door. He peered at Max suspiciously before asking him in. Then he led Max into a poorly lit room, on whose damp and stained walls hung portraits of white-bearded old men and of matrons with shawls covering their heads: Jews, as Max identified them.

With a magnifying glass, the merchant examined the jewels at length. The offer he then made was far below the going rate for jewels of similar, if not inferior, quality—Max knew, for he had been visiting jewelry stores. His blood boiled. What a grasping, miserly race! In this respect, at least, Hitler was right: the world would be better off without such grasping types.

"I should have known better," he said angrily, "what else can you expect from a Jew?"

With trembling fingers, he gathered up the jewels while the old man looked on in silence. He stood up and made for the door.

"One moment, Herr Max," the old man said in German. "We haven't closed our deal yet. Sit down, will you?"

Annoyed, Max hesitated but finally sat down.

"Let's engage ourselves in the ancient art of bargaining, an art still unknown in this country. Well, then, what I offered you was barely anything, right?"

Max couldn't fathom what the man was driving at.

"Barely anything, right?" insisted the old man.

"Yes," admitted Max, uneasy.

"So say it: That's barely anything."

Perplexed, Max sat there staring at him.

"Come on, say it!" the old man commanded.

"That's barely anything," said Max.

"They are my treasured possessions. . . ."

"They are my treasured possessions. . . ."

"I want more money for them."

"I want more money for them." Max rose to his feet. "Listen, if you're thinking that—"

"I'm not thinking anything," said the merchant dryly. "I heard what you said: That's barely anything, they're my treasured possessions, I want more money for them. Well, I'll double my offer."

Max stared openmouthed at the old man.

"I'll triple my offer. How's that? Three times as much?"

Now the amount was far more than what Max had hoped for. Astounded, he was at a loss for words.

"Are you satisfied?" asked the merchant. As Max made no reply, he persisted: "Are you satisfied?"

"Yes," mumbled Max.

"Louder, please."

"Yes!" Max shouted. "I'm satisfied."

The old man counted out the money.

"Check the amount, will you?"

"It's not necessary. . . ."

"Check it, will you? One shouldn't trust anybody. You should know that."

Max counted the money and put it in his pockets.

"Any complaints about the transaction?" the old man asked.

"No," said Max, grim.

"And will it upset you if"—a faint smile lit up the old man's wrinkled face—"I make a profit on the sale of these jewels that you treasure so much?"

"No," said Max.

"A hundred-percent profit? It won't upset you? What about a two-hundred-percent profit?"

"No."

"Good," said the old man, standing up. "Good-bye, then, Senhor Max. And be careful with your money."

Still bewildered, Max left. Once out in the street, he was stuck by sudden rage and felt like going back there and throwing the money at the man's face. But Max had already eaten humble pie that day. Besides, the thick rolls of money in his pockets began to create a pleasant sensation. He was rich! He had enough capital to set up a small business, maybe something classy like a bookstore or an art gallery; or he could go into real estate, live off the proceeds from the rent of his property, and devote all his time to studies and research work. Or he could invest the money in bonds and shares of stock, thus becoming richer and richer—after all, as Signor Ettore had said, Brazil was a country where people could strike it rich overnight. Yes, his prospects were excellent, and to celebrate, he decided to ask his landlady and her daughter out to dinner.

They made an evening of it. They chose a friendly little restaurant, which featured a smiling piano player. The food was excellent, the wine superb. They drank several toasts to the future, Max and the girl gazing at each other lovingly every time they raised their glasses. Max said that he intended to return to Germany, and that he would take the two of them with him and introduce them to his parents. His landlady, usually a reserved woman, was in high spirits, and even sang a song, accompanied by the pianist.

That night Max had a dream.

He was in a theater in Berlin, the same theater to which his mother used to take him when he was a boy. The only person in the audience, he was waiting impatiently for the play to start.

When the curtain went up, a grotesque dwarf appeared on the stage and announced that Wagner's opera *Parsifal* was going to be performed. A moment later, his father emerged. Draped in a long robe and wearing ludicrous makeup, he then opened his arms as if he were about to break into song, but instead, he proceeded to meow like a cat. How disgraceful, Max kept thinking, the tears running down his face. He wished his father would stop that folly, but no, he went on meowing, and he meowed nonstop until Max woke up.

But the meowing continued. Like the sea gull squealing above the dinghy, Max thought (but had there really been a sea gull?). He looked at the clock: it was twenty minutes past midnight. He got up and he went to the window.

The cat was nowhere in sight. However, it must be out there somewhere, probably in the backyard of the house next door, meowing loudly. Begone! shouted Max—a somewhat restrained shout, for he was in fact ashamed of the situation, which was, to a certain extent, ridiculous. Begone!

The cat continued to meow. Max repeated his command, this time in German. Nothing. Irritated, he picked up the first object within reach—his shoes—and hurled them into the backyard. The meowing stopped for a while only to start anew a moment later.

Max went back to bed and thrust his head under the pillows. In vain: the meowing resonated there as in a cavern. And it was no use plugging his ears, or crooning to himself: he could still hear the damn feline, whining away like an abandoned child. Finally, he fell asleep out of sheer exhaustion.

On the following day Max got up in a bad mood and with a headache. The worst, however, was the fact that now he had no shoes to wear. Peering through the window, he could see them out there in the neighbor's backyard, half-sunk in a puddle of water. Outside, it was pouring with rain. Obviously, going there to fetch them was out of the question. He decided to go out and buy a new pair. What's the matter, Herr Max? the landlady inquired upon seeing him in his slippers. My shoes were hurting my feet, he said, I'm going to buy new ones. And he slipped out before she could ask him any further questions.

The meowing recurred that night, and on the following night as well—but Max was well prepared, armed with a slingshot that he had bought from a kid in the neighborhood, and with a good supply of pebbles of assorted sizes. He was now all set to give chase to the cat, no matter where it was, and even at the risk of breaking roof tiles or windowpanes. It was actually with

impatience that he waited for the feline's serenade, and
barely had it started when Max leaped out of bed and
flung the window wide open. What he saw through the
open window of the house next door made him forget
all about the cat and its meowing.

A man stood looking at himself in the mirror.

Nothing wrong about a man looking at himself in the
mirror—if it weren't for the clothes that he was wearing:
a brown shirt, a black tie, knee-high boots. Max was
only too familiar with that attire; and as if this weren't
enough, the man was also wearing an armband on which
Max was able to identify the swastika. Alone in his bedroom, and without suspecting that someone could be
watching him at such a late hour—two o'clock in the
morning—the man was absorbed in enacting a curious
pantomime: he would raise his right arm; a moment
later, he would start gesticulating as if he were deliv-
ering a speech to a crowd; then, he would get closer to
the mirror and smile enticingly. After a period of time,
the man, having apparently grown tired of enacting this
scene, yawned, took off his clothes, carefully put them
away in the wardrobe, and then got into his pajamas.
The light went out and Max could see nothing else.

Max closed the window and sat down on the edge of
the bed. Even though the cat had stopped meowing, he
couldn't fall asleep—not after what he had witnessed.

A Nazi in Porto Alegre. A Nazi in the neighborhood.
A Nazi . . . Only one? One that he had seen, but how

many others were there in this district? In the city? In
Brazil, a country that had struck him as a paradise on
earth and that now appeared to be a threat to him?

However, he managed to pull himself together. *Relax,
Max, relax. No Nazi is watching you. You're the one who's
watching a Nazi.* But was the man really a Nazi? What
he had seen was a man in Nazi uniform engrossed in
grotesque gesticulations—which didn't necessarily
mean that he was *actually* a Nazi. He could be a person
with a covert or unacknowledged attraction to Nazism;
a person given to acting out his fantasies in the dead of
night.

Max took to watching the house next door. He saw
the man on various occasions, but never again in the
uniform. At times he was the loving parent who told
stories to his children (four of them, the oldest about
ten years old); or the thoughtful husband who brought
flowers to his wife; or the devoted son who asked his
elderly parents over for dinner, when he would open a
bottle of wine and drink to everybody's health; or the
fun-loving friend who invited his fellow workers to a
barbecue in his backyard. At times he was busy gar-
dening, at times he played with the dog, at times (usually on Sundays) he took a nap on the hammock, which
was hung between two shade trees. In short, this man
of average height, with a perfectly ordinary face, seemed
no different in any way from the rest of the neighbors.
Max even began to doubt the truth of what he had seen
that night. Once again he wondered if he was being the
victim of some hallucination, or it could have been just

another dream, one of the many that had been distressing him since childhood. He decided to forget the whole business and to stop looking through the window at night (even if the cat persisted in meowing nonstop). It would be wise for him to get some sleep. He started taking pills for this purpose.

After a few weeks he had forgotten (or almost forgotten) the incident and he felt reassured. But then there was a turn of events.

One day he had to go downtown. He had an appointment with a broker, a relative of his landlady's, whom she had recommended as an honest and competent person. Max wanted to find out about the possibilities of investing his money in the stock market; he was eager to engage in some sphere of activity; besides, he couldn't let his money remain idle.

As he was walking along Rua da Praia, his attention was caught by a small crowd gathered in the vicinity of Praça da Alfândega. He went in that direction.

It was a parade. Mostly young people—and all of them wearing a uniform similar to his neighbor's; all of them with their arms outstretched in the same kind of salute; all of them wearing an armband whose insignia, although not exactly like the swastika, as Max was now able to verify, was ominously reminiscent of the Nazi emblem.

Max hurried away. He was feeling sick—dizzy, nauseated. He entered a bar and sat down. The owner, solicitous, went up to him: Can I help you? Max asked for a glass of water. The man brought him the water, then looking outside, he remarked: Yeah, those guys make me sick, too, but it isn't worth getting in a stew about them. Max asked the man to send for a taxi. Upon arriving at his boardinghouse, he locked himself up in his room and lay down.

He had to think, to sort out his thoughts. He couldn't. The parade, the arrogant look of the young people, the outstretched arms, the flags, the drumrolls—the whole thing had upset him terribly. Naturally, he then knew nothing about *Integralismo*, the Brazilian right-wing movement that flourished in the 1930s, or about Plínio Salgado, its leader; later he was to learn about such things; but even so, he could guess that what he had seen was a typical Nazi demonstration, the minor variations possibly representing an adaptation of the Nazi doctrine to suit the countries of the New World. Anyhow, he felt insecure, as insecure and threatened as on the day he had left Germany, as insecure and threatened as during the days he had spent in the dinghy. Not even crossing the ocean and confronting the jaguar had saved him from his persecutors. Again: the city, which had seemed so friendly on that sunny morning, was now revealing its hidden dangers. He was even afraid of going back to his room, his habitual haven. How could he be sure that his landlady wasn't a sympathizer of Hitler? Or that her daughter wasn't a spy who had

hidden microphones under the novels of José de Alencar, her gentleness merely dissimulating the cold de-
termination of a secret agent?

No, he couldn't remain in Porto Alegre any longer.
But where could he go? Having no identification papers,
he wouldn't be able to leave the country. He would have
to find a small, remote place, still untouched by this
conflict. But where? He looked at the map of the state
of Rio Grande do Sul that he had hung on the wall in
order to familiarize himself with the names of its towns
and cities. Where would he go? In which region would
he feel more at home? Certainly not in the far south,
the region along the Uruguayan border—nothing but
huge holdings there, with gauchos galloping across
them—and he didn't even know how to ride on a horse.
The north or the northeast of the state would be more
congenial; he could buy a small plot of land there, and
among so many other immigrants already living in that
region, he would go unnoticed. While thinking about
such matters, he was feverishly packing his few be-
longings in a suitcase. He put on his overcoat and
descended the stairs. His landlady looked at him,
astonished.

"Are you leaving us, Senhor Max? So suddenly?"

"Urgent business," said Max. His voice came out
strange, choked. The woman said nothing, and merely
took the money proffered to her.

To say good-bye to Elizabeth proved to be even more
difficult. She, too, made no remarks, but it was with
great effort that she held back the tears. Max tried to

make a joke of the situation. After all, it wasn't going to be an eternal separation, it wasn't as if he were headed for another planet. He might soon be seeing them again, who knows.

On that same day, Max bought a car—a Model-A Ford—and he set out on his journey. Because the roads were bad and he was a mediocre driver—he had driven his father's old car only sporadically—he had to proceed slowly, stopping several times. But it was all right. He wanted to have plenty of time to explore the region, and above all, to think things over. The days were beautiful, and the journey pleasant, despite the dusty roads. Farm laborers would wave at him as he drove by, and he would reciprocate with enthusiasm and affection. Now that he was far away from the city and its sinister parades, he was beginning to feel well; and if he was all alone in the car, at least there was no threatening beast sitting beside him. No jaguar.

He was now in the mountains. Left behind were the populated areas. From now on, it would be only the mountains and the woods. Not the jungle about which Professor Kunz used to talk, but just the woods, which were, anyhow, dense and impenetrable—the habitat of exotic birds, of droll monkeys, and (a frisson of fear) of the Brazilian felines, or of some of them, at least. Max knew that the fauna of Rio Grande do Sul wasn't particularly rich in wild beasts, but his imagination took it upon itself to populate the forest with strange felines. Nevertheless, he drove on, headed for the unknown.

the

ONÇA

on the

HILLTOP

FOR days Max drove across the mountainous region. He was sure that he would find there the refuge that he had been searching for. In the city of Caxias do Sul, he negotiated the purchase of a property with a real-estate broker. The man looked like Signor Ettore, which left Max apprehensive. Was he entrusting his money to a swindler? But he soon swept aside his suspicions: the transaction was conducted in a legitimate way, all the papers were in order. It was Max who was in an irregular situation as an illegal immigrant. The real-estate broker showed understanding: for a modest sum of money, he obtained naturalization papers for

Max. Max Schmidt then became a Brazilian—and the owner of a piece of Brazilian land.

And a fine piece of land it was. A rather small farm by the standards of those days—two hundred and twenty hectares—but the land was fertile. With abundant water: two good versants. And there was a house, too—modest, with wattle walls, like all the other dwellings in the neighboring properties—but relatively comfortable; it even boasted electricity, supplied by a generator. The landscape was very beautiful: the property was on a high place, which afforded a view of the entire region. Only one place there was higher: a high, craggy hill covered with dense vegetation, known as Cerro Verde. Max's property ended at the foot of this hill.

It was with pride tinged with sadness that he settled in his new home. The sadness wasn't as great as the one he had felt upon leaving Germany; it was a softer, more resigned feeling. Melancholy. At an age when young people normally thought only of what they would do after graduating from college, Max was already a hardened, resigned man. His face, prematurely aged, showed the signs of the vicissitudes he had suffered: wrinkles, a bitter rictus. Nothing of what he had been through, however, mattered anymore. He wanted to start a new life. He didn't have the slightest idea what kind of life it was going to be, and it didn't matter. He would find out as the days, the weeks, the years went by.

There was, however, something that touched him:

the fact that he was close to the land. Notwithstanding his background in science, he was a mediocre agriculturist; with the help of a silent farmhand from the area, he planted grapevines, just as his neighbors did; he also cultivated a vegetable garden, and a corn patch; in addition, he raised pigs, chickens, rabbits, a few sheep, but nothing that yielded spectacular results, nothing that would earn him prizes in agricultural exhibitions. It wasn't he who had cultivated the giant pumpkin, winner of a silver medal in 1937; and the cucumber weighing 3.7 kilograms hadn't come from his vegetable garden either. However, it was possible for him to live off the land, and even to realize a moderate profit, which he found adequate. If after all that he had been through, some happiness was still in store for him, he didn't want to achieve it through money, but through simple things, such as watching the seeds sprout. His was a peaceful existence: he would wake up early in the morning, and drink *chimarrão*—the bitter unsweetened mate—with Injun, his employee; afterward, the two of them would work together. At first he had some difficulty getting used to the arduous toil, but in the course of time, his body hardened and he became as stalwart as any of the other settlers in the region. And like them, he learned how to examine the sky for signs of good or bad weather. He could tell from which direction the rain would come, and smell it while still in the distance.

In the evenings, however, after dinner—which Max himself prepared, as he did all his other meals—he would change into clean clothes and wear a necktie.

He would then sit down and listen to the records that he had ordered from Porto Alegre, the quiet valley resonating with the strains of Beethoven's Ninth Symphony. From Porto Alegre he also received books in both Portuguese and German. His library became famous among the settlers, who referred to him as "the Professor." His relationship with them was cordial but distant. Initially, he had thought that his life would always remain secluded, but little by little he began to feel the need to establish contact with cultured people, with whom he could discuss science and literature. Sometimes he would go to Caxias do Sul, there to attend a lecture or a concert. It was in that city that he first met a retired physician of Austrian descent, who lived with his wife in Canela, a small town nearby. Invited to visit them, Max hesitated, but ended up accepting the invitation. He then became a regular visitor to the couple's house.

Dr. Rudolf was an extraordinarily erudite man. For a long time he had practiced medicine in the region of the upper Uruguay River, where he had handled everything—general practice, surgery, obstetrics. He wished, however, that he had specialized in psychiatry. A self-taught psychoanalyst, he was well versed in the doctrines of Dr. Freud, with whom his father had worked in Vienna. He became interested in Max's accounts of Professor Kunz's researches, and he told Max about his own experiments with Brazilian Indians. He would gather the whole tribe together and tell them stories. One such story was about a young craftsman

named Ego, who made marvelous dolls, and his tormentors: Id, a foulmouthed, hairy dwarf (a creature
somewhat like the *curupira*, the bogeyman of the Brazilian forests—a mythical Indian with feet pointed back-
ward); and Super Ego, an aristocratic and authoritarian
master. After a day of grueling work, Ego would lie
down, but he was unable to fall asleep: Id would then
come from the basement and proceed to dance around
Ego's cot, making obscene faces at him. Ego would get
up and follow the dwarf across the fields until they came
to what looked like the entrance to an armadillo's bur-
row, but was in fact the entrance to the fabulous sub-
terranean palace of the fairy Morgana. As he stood in
the huge, torch-lit halls, Ego would marvel at the sight
of the young, blond women that were dancing naked.
They would extend their arms to him, but as the young
man was about to throw himself upon them, in would
come Super Ego, in his cutaway coat and top hat, his
lips a thin line. At a signal from his silver-topped cane,
the dancers would vanish. He would then turn to poor
Ego, and take him to task, repeating in a monotone: *Thou
shalt not sin, thou shalt not sin.* The story always ended
on a deliberately optimistic note, with Ego succeeding
in freeing himself from his tormentors and marrying the
fairy Morgana.

Such stories delighted the Indians, who preferred
them to the stories from the Bible, or the ones about
Tupã—the Christian God. (*Tupã* was the word for
"thunder" in the Tupian Indian language until the Jesuit
missionaries started using it to designate the Christian

God.) One of the Indians, an imaginative sculptor, carved in wood the figures of Ego, Id, and Super Ego, which reinforced the therapeutic effect of the narratives. Young Indian males afflicted with infinite sadness, and hysterical Indian girls would heal themselves by making propitiatory offerings to those idols.

Max would listen to those accounts with interest mingled with a certain uneasiness. He, too, regarded himself as being a kind of Ego; he, too, kept tossing and turning in bed at night, unable to fall asleep, goaded as he was by the urges of sex. Every once in a while, a certain Margarete, a cabaret dancer in Caxias do Sul, would come to his place. A blond, cheerful young woman, she reminded him somewhat of Frida. Most of the time, however, he was in dire need of a woman—another source of anguish, as if he didn't have enough anguish already.

And then he was taken ill.

He became seriously ill with a fever that, for Dr. Rudolf, had no apparent cause. He had to be hospitalized; he was submitted to many tests, nothing wrong was found, but his condition kept worsening by the day. Delirious, he would ramble on about his parents, about Harald, about a jaguar. The doctors had already given up on him and considered his case closed, when he took a turn for the better. The fever broke, he became lucid again, but he was very weak. So weak that he could barely walk. He wanted to go home at all cost. Injun, his silent employee, suggested getting someone to do the cooking and the housework for him. And he took his niece to Max's place.

Upon first seeing this girl, this Jaci, Max didn't pay much attention to her—in fact, he was in no condition to notice her. However, as he convalesced from his illness, his interest in her began to grow.

She was nineteen years old. An Indian type, naturally, but an exceedingly beautiful type—the kind of Indian woman portrayed by José de Alencar in his novels. Max liked her; he liked her slightly goofy manner, the simple songs that she intoned while preparing a meal. It was in the kitchen that he kissed her for the first time; on the following night, naturally, she slept with him, and from then on, she didn't return to her house.

At first Max was a bit frightened—wouldn't Jaci's relatives come storming into the house, shouting: Return the girl to us, you degenerate? But no. Nothing like that happened. Jaci's parents were dead, and Injun, her next of kin, seemed indifferent to, if not pleased with, what was going on: after all, Jaci had never had it so good, and Injun had even arrogated to himself certain privileges—he was working less, and once in a while he would help himself to a bottle of wine from the cupboard, in compensation for his role as a go-between in the affair.

Max loved her.

It was difficult for him to come to this realization,

partly because he was beset by fear, partly because he had become hard-boiled, but also partly because he hadn't entirely given up the idea of returning to Germany, there to marry a young woman he hadn't met yet, a young woman who in his dreams was very different from Jaci, more like the daughter of his former landlady. For all these reasons, he had not fallen in love with her at first sight, as it happens in the movies. What he felt for her blossomed gradually. By stages: she, at the window, absentminded, looking at the rain falling outside; she, crooning to herself while arranging the flowers in a vase; she, crying quietly, heaven knows why. . . . First, tenderness, soon followed by love. Max was certain that it was love. He could no longer live without her. And he stopped thinking of Germany, or hardly ever thought of it. Jaci was now all that mattered to him; they spent almost all their time together: in the vegetable garden, or strolling in the fields, or looking at Cerro Verde enveloped in a thin mist, or staying home by the hot oven, where sweet potatoes were baking. They smiled more often than they talked. She found his heavy accent funny, but she was also ashamed of the way she spoke: I don't know how to talk like a professor, the way you do. To her, Max was a professor, there was no arguing about it; to her, he was a man who knew many complicated things that were too hard for her to understand. Like Germany, or Nazism, which she couldn't fathom. But she liked his story about the jaguar, and she laughed heartily upon hearing about

Max's tribulations aboard the dinghy, and not once did it occur to her that the whole thing could have been just delirium or imagination. She had once heard of a similar case, of a fisherman who went aboard his canoe, where he found an enormous snake. Paralyzed by terror, he couldn't avert his eyes from the ophidian, and his boat, carried by the current, drifted for many kilometers until it ran aground, at which point the snake disappeared amid the vegetation of the riverbank.

And they made love. In the beginning it wasn't always good—she, somewhat clumsy; gradually, however, they learned about each other, and lovemaking became better every time.

When Jaci found out that she was pregnant, Max didn't hesitate for one moment: he went to the registry office and set a date for their wedding. He didn't intend to have a party (it would pointless, what with his parents being so far away), but he wanted the ceremony to convey some significance. So he asked Dr. Rudolf and his wife if they would act as the best man and the matron of honor. Taken by surprise, the doctor agreed; however, when Max went to their house a few days later to see about some final arrangements, the doctor lapsed into silence. No, he didn't know if he would be able to attend the wedding, his wife was indisposed.

"But I've just spoken to her," said Max, surprised.

Dr. Rudolf hesitated.

"Listen, Max," he said finally. "I'd better level with you. My wife doesn't want you to come here anymore.

I hope you understand. Some people have . . . problems with . . . you know. There's nothing I can do, she can't help feeling the way she does."

Max couldn't understand. What have I done? he was about to ask, but then it dawned on him. It had nothing to do with him, Jaci was the problem. The girl with the dark skin. The Indian girl.

Max looked at the doctor sitting in his comfortable living room. His eyes lowered, he was nervously drumming his fingers on the arms of the chair. (A sudden curiosity: had Dr. Rudolf ever told his wife about Ego's dream? No. Probably not.) Max rose to his feet and left.

His daughter, Hildegarde (later shortened to Hilde), was born in August 1939. A month later the war broke out. Max went through a period of considerable anxiety; on the one hand, he hoped that the Nazis would be defeated; on the other hand, he feared for his parents' safety. Daily he would follow the news from the front, looking at the map of Europe before him. Jaci was worried: her husband didn't sleep well, he talked in his sleep. However, the child demanded her full attention, and so all she could do was to tell Max to relax, things probably weren't as bad as they looked.

His daughter. Ah, yes, his daughter. Gradually Max began to forget about the war—the war and everything else—because he had eyes only for his Hilde. In his journal he wrote only about her: Today Hilde drank juice for the first time, today she laughed, today she cut her first tooth, today she said Mummy, today she took her first step, today she said something funny (there

were many funny things: they filled pages and pages).
Thus, time marched on without Max even noticing.
However, the premature baldness that he had inherited
from his father became more pronounced; in 1940 several of his teeth had to be pulled out; in 1941 he was
bedridden with rheumatic pains for several days. What
do you expect, Dr. Rudolf would say, one day you'll
be old and sick, it's inevitable. Max didn't really believe
that it would happen to him; he felt fine. A sunburnt
man. Used to inclemencies.

In 1942 Brazil declared war on Germany. A few weeks
after the announcement was made, Max drove his old
truck to Caxias do Sul, where he would be making a
few deliveries. He parked in front of a grocery store;
when he got out of the truck, some young men hanging
around looked at him in a strange way. Ignoring them,
Max entered the store. Upon coming out half an hour
later, he saw that black swastikas had been painted on
his truck. The young men were nowhere to be seen.

Max flex into a rage. He went to the middle of the
street.

"I'm not a Nazi!" he kept shouting. "I hate the Nazis,
and I hate whoever did this to my truck. Show your
face here if you're brave enough!"

Nobody came. Finally, Max got into his truck and
drove off. From then on he wouldn't go into town; the
shopkeepers had to come to his farm to buy his produce.

In addition, he stopped listening to the radio and reading the newspapers.

One day he learned that the war had ended. His first thought was for his parents: now he would be able to visit them. And immediately, the questions: Were they still alive? What had become of them?

He decided to go to Germany. His wife encouraged him: Go, Max, go and visit your folks. Bring me a present? Hilde asked. Max smiled, overcome with emotion. He would return to Germany, yes, but only as a visitor. *His folks* were here, in Brazil: Jaci and his daughter. They were the only ones he really cared about.

Taking his savings from the bank, he bought a ticket to Germany and set off on his journey. It wasn't easy to enter Berlin; he had to talk to the occupation authorities, produce documents. Finally, he was issued with a safe conduct that allowed him to enter the city.

It was with deep emotion and a great deal of sadness that Max returned to Berlin. Nothing remained of the city of his childhood days. Buildings razed to the ground, people wandering about the streets like sleepwalkers—a nightmarish atmosphere. His father's store—the first place where he went—was a huge pile of rubble. Picking his way amid the debris, he saw something glittering in the sun. It was a glass eye. The eye from the stuffed tiger. He wrapped it carefully in his handkerchief and put it into his pocket.

His old house was gone, too—destroyed in the bomb-

ing. As he stood there, looking at the ruins, a woman
with a hobbling gait and a slightly deranged look in her
eyes approached him and asked for a cigarette. Max
recognized her as one of their neighbors.

"Don't you remember me, Frau Herta?"

Frightened, she looked at him. A moment later a smile
opened her face.

"But it's Max! Little Max!"

In tears, she hugged him. "What a misfortune, Max.
What a terrible misfortune, Max. Why did we do this,
Max?"

She took him home, or to what remained of it—just
one room with a piece of canvas serving as a door—
made him sit down, offered him what little she had—
some tea, a few hard crackers. Max was anxious to ask
about the fate of his parents, but she anticipated his
questions.

"Your mother died, Max. She died soon after you
went away. And your father was committed to an asylum, Max. He went crazy. A lot of people went
crazy. . . . An awful lot."

As he took his leave, Max gave her his cigarettes, and
then he headed for the asylum, which happened to be
in the vicinity. It was a wretched place—a cluster of
buildings half-fallen to ruins—among which patients
dressed in rags were strolling. Max introduced himself
to a nurse, who looked him up and down before she
took him to one of the wards.

Max didn't recognize his father. The hulking man
with the arrogant air was now reduced to a thin old

man, bald and toothless, who sat muttering unintelligible words, with his eyes fixed on the floor. Sitting down by his side, Max hugged him and stroked his furrowed face. It's me, Father, he said in a low voice, your son, Max. Hans made no reply. It's useless, said the nurse, he's a vegetable. Without saying anything, Max got up. As he was about to leave, his father grabbed him, making him bend down.

"All of this, Herr General," he whispered in Max's ear, "has to do with Jews. I should know, I used to be in the fur business. Listen to my advice, and release the tigers."

Max kissed him on the face. The nurse saw him to the door. He told her that he would be sending his father a monthly allowance and gave her his address in Brazil. Finally, he tipped her generously, which made her break into a smile and turn suddenly pleasant: Don't worry, Herr Max, we'll look after your father well. Then lowering her voice: I'm afraid he won't last much longer, poor soul. . . . But until he goes to his resting place, we'll provide him with every possible comfort. We'll let you know when he passes away.

Max shook the proffered hand and left.

He walked along the streets of Berlin. He came to a bar where he and his father used to go for a beer; it had escaped destruction and was open for business. Max went in and took a seat. He was the only customer there. A gloomy old man waited on him.

"There's only tea, sir. Tea and mineral water."

Max ordered tea. As he sat there, slowly sipping his tea, he noticed that a woman on the street had stopped at the door and was looking at him attentively. He rose to his feet at the same time that she came running into the bar.

"Max!"

It was Frida: this ugly, fat woman, this aged, shabbily dressed woman was Frida, whom he used to kiss in the stockroom amid the furs. They held each other for a long time, she in tears, as the waiter, indifferent, looked on. She would let go of him for a moment—Max! It's been such a long time, Max!—and then hug him again. Finally, they both sat down. Max offered her tea; then, after a moment's hestiation, he asked her if she would like to have something to eat. Yes, she would. The waiter brought them what was available—an omelette, some bread, which she ate with a ravenous appetite. And she talked on and on, with her mouth full, telling him all about the war years, terrible years they had been, with unimaginable hardships. Max noticed the slightly faded photograph on the medallion that she wore round her neck. And what about that husband of yours? he asked.

She shrugged her shoulders.

"I have no idea. He disappeared during the war. I think he ran away. Many did . . . But I couldn't care less. You know, Max, I never liked him."

Then, leaning forward, her cheeks greasy from the food she had eaten, she took his hand in hers.

"I did like you a lot, Max. Those afternoons in the stockroom . . . remember?"

She gave a little laugh. Then, turning serious, she looked steadily at him, her lips parted, her nostrils suddenly dilated by desire.

"Oh, Max, it's been such a long time. . . . Would you like to . . . ?"

He hesitated—just for a brief moment, but she noticed, and it was humiliating enough. She bridled.

"Oh, never mind. Anyhow, there's no time, I must rush now. I have an appointment."

She stood up and extended a stiff hand, which he tried to hold in his, but she didn't let him. I hope we'll bump into each other again, she said, and went away. Max watched her walk hurriedly across the street. She then disappeared around the corner.

Max returned to Brazil the same way he had traveled to Germany—by ship. It was a large passenger ship, with every possible amenity. He had a decent cabin in the tourist class. There were no howling animals, and the risk of a shipwreck seemed remote: the ship was equipped with all kinds of safety devices, and the captain inspired trust in the passengers. If at night he couldn't sleep well, if he awoke startled and in a cold sweat, it was probably because he was in the middle of the ocean, far away from home, far away from his wife and daughter, far away from his bed, to which he had gown used. I'll never travel again, he decided. Neither to Germany, nor to anywhere else.

·   ·   ·

Max resumed his routine on the farm. He would plant,
harvest, look after the animals; evenings, he would read
and listen to music. Jaci kept complaining: You never
take me to the movies, Max. I've been to the movies
only twice in my whole life!

Max thought she needed another child. Her preg-
nancy, however, ended in a miscarriage, and Jaci had
to be hospitalized because of the hemorrhage. Max left
Hilde with the servant and stayed with his wife at the
hospital for almost a month. Upon returning home, he
was surprised to see that a house was being built on the
very top of Cerro Verde. It was a strange place to build
a house, for it was almost inaccessible; and by the looks
of it, it was going to be a luxurious mansion. Do you
know who's building it? Max asked Injun. His employee
didn't know. Max got hold of his binoculars, and from
then on he watched the construction work.

At first he saw only the workers, the foreman, the
engineer; one day, however, he caught sight of someone
who might be the owner. His back was turned to Max;
a man of a certain age, elegantly attired, a European
type, for sure. The man turned around and Max tried
to focus on his face. As soon as he saw it clearly, he felt
a thud in his chest, and it seemed that his heart had
stopped beating: he knew that face, he had seen it before—and not too long ago. On Frida's medallion: it
was her husband. Max was now frantically adjusting
the binoculars, trying to take a good look at the man.
But at that moment he got into his car, drove away in
haste, and was gone.

Ever since that day Max was no longer the same. His
wife, still convalescing, had to worry about him: work
had lost its appeal for him, he had no appetite, he slept
poorly, and kept moaning in his sleep. Even little Hilde
noticed that something must be going on: What's wrong
with Daddy? she would ask, but Jaci didn't have an
answer. Go and see the doctor, she kept saying to her
husband. In reply, Max assured her that he didn't need
a doctor, he was fine. But Jaci knew that this wasn't
the case; and to make matters even worse, she thought
that she was the cause of the problem: You don't like
me anymore, Max, she would whimper. You've grown
tired of me because I'm not white, because I'm not of
your race, you want someone blond, Max, isn't that so?
Upset, Max would leave the house.

He would wander across the fields, haunted by ancient ghosts, obsessed by the face he had seen through
the binoculars. Constantly brooding about this matter,
he would despair. Why wouldn't they leave him alone,
these accursed recollections? He had started a new life,
he didn't want to remember the past. What did it matter
if Frida's husband was still alive, if he was living in
Brazil, and as luck would have it, not far from his farm?

But it mattered, yes. Max knew that it mattered.

It was imperative that he find out the truth; that he
go to the lair of the wild beast; that he confront it in its
own stronghold. But how? And under what pretext?

While he was still wrestling with such questions, the
house was finished and the man moved in. Apparently,
he lived alone and had no family, but there were two

other people living in the house: a man, probably a servant, and a woman who always wore an apron—the cook. They looked after the house during the owner's frequent absences, which made it hard for Max to plan on a visit. However, he found out that the man was always home on the weekends. Thus, on a Saturday, Max drove there in his truck.

Access to the property was through a narrow graveled road, undoubtedly built by the owner of the house, for his was the only dwelling in that area. Max came to a stop before the big iron gate. It was locked. A sign said: *Private property. Beware. Fierce dogs.* And indeed, there were four mastiffs, barking furiously.

Max honked his horn. The servant appeared.

"What is it?" he asked, distrustful.

"I'm the owner of the farm down below," explained Max. "I'm here to pay a visit to the owner of the house."

After hesitating for a while, he added with a forced smile: "To extend a warm welcome to him. It's the custom here in this neck of the woods."

Without saying a word, the servant turned around. A while later he was back. He drove the dogs away and opened the gate.

"Come with me, please."

Max was taken to the house, but before he stepped in, the servant said: "Your boots. Please clean them on the doormat."

Max obeyed, but with reluctance. The servant then

showed him into an elegant study. The furniture, locally made, was rustic, and rustic, too, were the woolen carpets; but there were paintings and sculptures galore; the ashtrays were made of crystal, and the books on the shelves were lavishly bound. Max looked at the titles: novels, books on philosophy; nothing of a compromising nature.

"Good morning! What can I do for you?"

There he was, all smiles, the man that Max had been watching through his binoculars. Casually but elegantly dressed in a tweed jacket, flannel trousers, a silk scarf around his neck. Affable, pleasant; and bearing no resemblance to the portrait of the man on Frida's medallion. But then, thought Max, time passes. Even for a bastard like this man, time passes. Indignation mounted in Max's chest, and involuntarily, he clenched his fists. But he managed to control himself, and with difficulty he introduced himself, saying that he was there to make a friendly call on his neighbor.

"In this case, welcome to my home," the man said in a heavily accented Portuguese. Actually, he seemed self-conscious about his accent, and after some vacillation he asked if he could carry on the conversation in German. Max, too, hesitated, but he replied in the affirmative. The man then introduced himself as Georges Backhaus, a retired merchant from Berlin, now living on the proceeds of his investments.

"I decided to end my days in Brazil." A sorrowful smile. "I got fed up with Europe, fed up with war and destruction."

The impudence of this fellow, Max was thinking. What an impudent, treacherous, murderous man. But a real con artist, too, Max had to admit. He played the role of citizen of the world wonderfully well.

"A liqueur?"

Max made no reply. The man filled two small glasses and proffered Max one of them, the smile never leaving his face.

Fired with a sudden rage, Max threw the glass on the floor. His host recoiled, startled.

"That's it! Enough of this shit!"

Alarmed, the man stood looking at Max.

"Don't you know who I am?" bellowed Max. "Max! Max Schmidt! The lover of your wife Frida. Of the wife you deserted! The friend of Harald, of the Harald whom you denounced to the police! And who killed himself because of you, you rotten shitheel!"

"I don't know what you're talking about," said the man, livid. "And please control yourself, or I'll have to ask you to leave my house."

The servant put his head around the door.

"Is there anything you need, Senhor Georges?"

"No, thanks. I'll call you if I do."

The door closed. Backhaus turned to Max.

"This is most unpleasant, Senhor Max. But I think I can understand your anger: you must have mistaken me for someone else. Those of us who left Germany—"

Max cut him short.

"Like hell I have." His tone of voice was low but

threatening. "And I don't intend to leave things as they are. Soon you and I are going to square accounts. So long."

Without waiting for a reply, Max walked out, slamming the door behind him. Under the vigilant and distrustful eyes of the servant, he climbed into his truck, swerved it viciously onto the flower beds of the property—Watch out! shouted the servant, you're ruining the plants!—and drove away.

Now he knew what he had to do. He would devote himself to unmasking this Nazi, and not rest until he was arrested and sentenced.

He went to Porto Alegre and headed straight for a police station. I want to report a serious fact, he said to the chief of police who had received him in his office. The man listened to him attentively and made notes. After a while he interrupted Max, who was in the middle of his convoluted story.

"Do you have any proof to substantiate your accusation?"

"Proof?" Max creased his forehead. "Who needs proof? I'm telling you everything that happened! This man is a Nazi! A militant Nazi! Isn't my word good enough?"

The chief of police smiled.

"Well, that's not it. You see, I need concrete facts. Documents, photographs . . ."

Max sat staring at him, perplexed.

"No," he mumbled. "I don't have anything like that."

Suddenly the face of the chief of police struck him as being familiar.

"I think I recognize you," he said, "but I can't place you."

The chief of police was also looking at Max curiously.

"Well, I think I know you, too. . . ."

After thinking for a while, he added: "Didn't you use to live in a boardinghouse in Floresta in 1937 or 38?"

Of course: it was the man in the uniform. The one who had exhibited himself in front of the mirror. Now the whole thing made sense to Max: the chief of police would never investigate a complaint against a Nazi. And what's more: perhaps those two men knew each other, perhaps they were in cahoots. Max rose abruptly to his feet and left.

Convinced that he would get nowhere through the legal channels (the man has connections, he is probably well protected), Max decided to pursue some other— but riskier—route. He wrote an article and had it published as a paid advertisement in the *Correio do Povo* (a copy of which he had seen in the house of the fake Georges Backhaus), under the headline A NEST OF SNAKES IN OUR HILLY REGIONS. *On the top of Cerro Verde,* began the piece, *is a beautiful, newly built house,* and it went on in this vein, ending with a statement about the house being the hideout of a Nazi with a hideous past.

This time he succeeded in getting his neighbor's goat. On the day following the publication of his piece in the newspaper, Backhaus's servant came to his house.

"My boss sent me here to tell you to stop this non-sense. He doesn't want to take action, but if you persist, you'll feel sorry."

"Get out of here!" yelled Max. But he was now pleased: he had succeeded in provoking the beast, in luring him away from his lair. He would have to vex the Nazi even more, make him fly off the handle, goad him into committing some folly. Leave him alone, entreated Jaci, who had witnessed the scene with alarm. You'll get into trouble with this man.

Max, however, wasn't going to give up. Not now that he had devised a plan. On that very night he launched an attack. He went to the property on Cerro Verde, succeeded in gaining access to the grounds—but first he had to poison the dogs—and as the day was dawning, he climbed up to the roof, where he hoisted a crudely made Nazi flag: a bedsheet on which he had painted the swastika. He then returned to his farm, from where, even without the binoculars, he could see the flag fluttering in the wind. And certainly, so could anyone who happened to be passing on the road. It would be impossible to come up with a better way of denouncing the man. And apparently, it wasn't until late in the afternoon that Georges Backhaus noticed the existence of the flag. Max grinned while watching the arrogant servant balancing himself precariously on the roof as he tried to remove the flag. But Jaci worried. That's enough now, Max, you've taken your revenge. Max, however, was already engineering his next raid. He had plenty of ideas: he could disseminate pamphlets about the Nazi, he could write a play, he could compose songs.

He didn't have a chance to execute any of these plans. On the following day at dawn, he woke up with someone pounding vigorously on the door. It was Injun, scared out of his wits.

"Come and see, boss!"

Max followed him to the rabbit hutches. What he saw was enough to turn his stomach: the cages smashed, the rabbits, badly mauled, strewn all over the place, pools of blood on the ground. It was the onça, said Injun.

He was referring to a story that had been circulating in the region, according to which, an onça—a *panthera onça*, the fiercest Brazilian wildcat—was at large in Cerro Verde, having escaped from a truck that was taking it to a private zoo in Porto Alegre.

An onça? No. To Max, this was the work of a creature far more vicious than any wildcat. But if Georges Backhaus intended to intimidate him in this way, he would never succeed. No matter how many rabbits he killed.

Max had his article reprinted in the *Correio do Povo*, and then he made ready for any eventuality: he, Injun, and a youth who also worked for Max, took turns watching over his property at night. He gave each a gun and ammunition and told them to shoot at anything that moved.

"Even if it's people, do you hear?"

He thought for a moment and then added: "Especially if it's people."

On his first night of vigil Max recalled his father hunting tigers in India: but he wasn't in the least keen on setting up that kind of ambush. The thought of the Nazi now taking the offensive enraged him; however, the conflict between the two of them had turned into a kind of game. Max had made the last move; it was now Georges Backhaus's turn.

But he, apparently, had nothing to do with the dead animals. For two weeks they were on the watch—but nothing happened. Injun started to complain: he was old, there was no way he could spend the whole night without any sleep; the youth, who suffered from bronchitis, threatened to quit his job; as for Jaci, she would open the window in the middle of the night and shout: "Come to bed, Max. Enough of this nonsense!"

Max had no choice but to give up his scheme to maintain vigilance. He was certain, however, that the onça— Backhaus—would be attacking soon. And he decided to provoke him: he had his article published for a third time. Then he awaited his neighbor's reaction. What would the target be this time? The chickens? The beds of lettuce?

A few days later Max was summoned to appear before the court. Jaci accompanied him to Caxias do Sul. In the courtroom he was advised to hire a lawyer. Georges Backhaus had started a lawsuit against him because of the articles in the newspaper.

Throughout the return trip home Max remained silent. He was ruminating over thoughts of revenge, and at the same time, he was being assailed by forebodings.

He was convinced that he was confronting a dangerous, unpredictable enemy, far more cunning than he had imagined (until then his idea of the man had corresponded exactly with Frida's description of her husband, a man whose intelligence she used to deride). It would take more than spiteful taunts to defeat such an enemy. The first was far more serious than he had realized.

No sooner had Max and Jaci arrived at the farm than they noticed that something was amiss: Injun's shirt lay discarded on the ground, and from the front door of the house, the youth was signaling nervously to them.

They got out of the truck and went running into the house. Injun met them halfway.

"The onça, boss! The onça struck again. Bad luck, boss!"

He then proceeded to tell them how they had come upon little Hilde, lying unconscious in the woods, her clothes torn, her body covered with cuts and grazes. Upon hearing this, Jaci started to scream. Max picked up his daughter, carried her to the truck, and drove in the direction of the hospital.

They stayed awake all night in the hospital's waiting room. In the morning the doctor came to see them and told them not to worry, the girl was fine.

"How did she hurt herself like that? Was it thorns?"

"No," said Max. "I don't think it was thorns." He hesitated, then asked the doctor if the girl had said anything about the incident. "No," said the doctor, "she doesn't remember anything."

Thank goodness, thought Max. Thank goodness she can't remember. Leaving Jaci at the hospital, he returned home.

With methodical calmness, he set about making all the necessary preparations. First, he wrote a letter, not to Jaci, who could barely read, but to Dr. Rudolf, telling him not to be surprised at his behavior; he was acting calmly, in full possession of all his faculties, convinced that he was doing his duty. Then he asked the doctor to help Jaci put her affairs in order, after which he thanked him for everything.

After putting the letter into an envelope, Max went to the toolshed. He stood there, hesitating for a while: he took hold of a sickle, examined it, his brow creased, a wan smile on his lips, and then put it aside; the same procedure with an ax; finally he opted for a large knife, the largest he had—a fish knife with an eighty-centimeter-long blade. He got into his truck and drove off, headed for Cerro Verde. He stopped some five hundred meters from his enemy's house. From there he would proceed on foot.

The gate wasn't locked. No sooner had he opened it than he heard barking. It was the dog—the only one, a Dalmatian—replacing the mastiffs. It came running and then it leaped up at Max, who slashed at it with the large fish knife while it was still in midair. The animal, its skull cracked, fell to the ground, as if struck by lightning. A shrill scream: it was the cook, who had been watching the scene and was now fleeing to the woods.

As for the male servant, he was nowhere in sight—his day off, perhaps. Or perhaps he, too, had run away.

Max cast a glance at the dead dog. Unhurriedly, he made for the house. The door was open. Knife in hand, he went in.

There was nobody in the study, nor in the living room. He opened a door that led to a long corridor, at the end of which stood Georges Backhaus.

He was wielding a gun, naturally. Max walked up to him, his eyes fixed on the other man's hand. Not because of the weapon, though. Because of the fingernails. Judging from what he could discern in the dim light, the fingernails weren't long. Neither were they pointed. Besides, there was no blood on them, but Max knew that blood could be washed off with water. Nothing abnormal in that hand. Except for the gun. Stop, ordered the man in a muffled voice. When Max didn't, he pulled the trigger.

The bullet hit him on the left shoulder, and the impact threw him to the floor. Almost immediately, he picked himself up, and indifferent to the pain and the blood that was oozing warmly down his chest, he continued to walk. Another gunshot, and this time the bullet merely grazed his left arm, but even so, what terrible pain. Max stopped walking for a moment, but only for a moment, before he continued to advance, tightening his grip on the fish knife.

Smiling, Georges Backhaus turned the weapon on himself. He hesitated, as if about to say something, but soon afterward he pulled the trigger. And he fell down without a sound.

Leaving the place, Max went straight to the police. He had to be hospitalized, naturally, but as soon as he was discharged from the hospital, he was arrested and later went on trial. When asked if he had killed Georges Backhaus, he replied in the affirmative. Why did he do it? Because of a debt, he replied in his terse deposition. Considering the fact that he had been wounded, as well as his good conduct, which was confirmed by all the witnesses, the judge sentenced him to six years in prison, notwithstanding the protests of the public prosecutor, a dog lover who was particularly outraged by the death of the Dalmatian ("Your Honor should take into account the criminal potentiality of an individual who, in cold blood, kills a poor dog that was only doing its duty").

Max was taken to the penitentiary in Porto Alegre. A model prisoner, he spent his time reading and working in the prison's vegetable garden; he never picked a fight with anyone and never got into trouble. Because of his good behavior, he was released on parole before his sentence expired. Upon his release, he returned to the farm, where everything had run smoothly during his absence.

From then on Max led a tranquil life. He got along well with everybody, but he refused to talk about his past,

partly because he had really forgotten what had happened to him—just like Hilde, who was unable to recall
what had happened to her on the day she was found
collapsed in the woods. It was perhaps for this reason
that she was a high-strung young woman; nevertheless,
she graduated from normal school, married an engineer,
and gave birth to four children, who were the joy of old
Jaci.

In the last years of his life, Max devoted himself to
raising pedigree cats—a special breed of Angora cats
("Brazilian angoras"), which won prizes in various cat
shows. Very docile, and with an unusual sensitivity,
these animals would purr softly when Max sang them
lullabies, and they expressed a particular preference for
children.

Max Schmidt died in 1977. I'm at peace with my felines,
he would say in his last days, but nobody knew exactly
what he meant. But it was just that: Max was, finally,
at peace with his felines.